"Is that all you intend to do, watch?"

demanded Poker Angie after she had shed her clothes.

He reached behind him to lock the door, then unbuckled his gunbelt and began to undress.

"God," she said when he was naked. "I'd almost forgotten what a huge bastard you are."

And she meant that in more ways than one.

As he moved to take her in his arms he was reminded of how tall she was. Tracker was six-four, and Poker Angie was still more than an armful for him...

"Let's stop wasting time," she gasped eagerly, pulling him towards the bed.

Avon Books are available at special quantity discounts for bulk purchases for sales promotions, premiums, fund raising or educational use. Special books, or book excerpts, can also be created to fit specific needs.

For details write or telephone the office of the Director of Special Markets, Avon Books, Dept. FP, 1790 Broadway, New York, New York 10019, 212-399-1357.

TOM CUTTER

TRACKER •4

CHINATOWN CHANCE

▲ AVON
PUBLISHERS OF BARD, CAMELOT, DISCUS AND FLARE BOOKS

CHINATOWN CHANCE is an original publication of Avon
Books. This work has never before appeared in book form.

AVON BOOKS
A division of
The Hearst Corporation
1790 Broadway
New York, New York 10019

First Avon Printing, October, 1983

AVON TRADEMARK REG. U. S. PAT. OFF. AND IN
OTHER COUNTRIES, MARCA REGISTRADA, HECHO EN
U. S. A

Printed in the U. S. A.

WFH   10   9   8   7   6   5   4   3   2   1

To Hom Fee Yuen

Historical Note

In San Francisco of the 1880s, the most popular games in Chinese casinos were fan-tan, and *pak kop piu,* which means "white pigeon ticket."

White pigeon ticket was named for pieces of paper about five inches square, upon which were printed the first eighty characters of the *Ts'intsz'man,* or *Thousand Character Classic.* As its name implies, this book contains one thousand characters, no two of which are the same. In a typical white pigeon ticket lottery, a customer purchased an eighty-character ticket for one dollar, and on it he checked ten characters at random. He then submitted his ticket to the agent he bought it from and awaited a drawing, held twice a day, in which twenty out of the eighty characters on the ticket were selected. If the customer "caught" five of the characters, he was paid $2.00. If he had six, he made $20.00; seven, $200.00; and so on up to ten, for which he made $3,000. The tickets could be purchased for as little as ten cents, which is why it was such a popular game among the California Chinese—although the game was by no means restricted to Chinese. It is estimated that "whites" invested far more than three million dollars a year in it.

The game got its name because the lottery was illegal in China, and professional gamblers used carrier pigeons to convey the tickets and winning numbers between their offices, rather than take the risk of being arrested while carrying the tickets on them.

As far as I know, there was no White Pigeon Tong.

THE AUTHOR

Prologue

When Ah Ching turned the corner and entered Ross Alley, his heart began to beat uncomfortably fast within his breast. The closer he got to his meeting with Loo Quon, the head of the White Pigeon Tong, the more frightened he became.

It was beginning to grow dark, and Ross Alley was teeming with late-evening customers for the illegal Chinese gambling parlors—the ones that the White Pigeon paid the police many dollars to protect. Ah Ching ran one of the tong's Dupont Street fan-tan parlors, and it was for this reason that he was on his way to meet with Loo Quon. The news that he had for the tong head was not good, and he knew that it might very well cost him *his* head. Not reporting it, however, could result in the most painful death possible, and he would rather lose his head swiftly than die that way.

When he reached the mouth of the small alley that led to Loo Quon's place he stopped, wiped the perspiration from his brow with his sleeve, then continued on into the alley. He walked to the end, where he came to a door and knocked. When the eyehole slot in the door opened and a pair of eyes appeared, the frightened Chinaman said, "Ah Ching."

The eyes looked him over once, then the slot closed. He heard the bolts being thrown on the inside to unlock the door, and then it swung inward to admit him.

"You smell of fear," Hom Lu Sin told him. Known as Lu Hom in Ross Alley, he was Loo Quon's number one boy. He was a small man, but he frightened Ah Ching almost as much as the tong leader himself. Ah Ching had seen the little Chinaman take apart much bigger men with his bare hands—and enjoy it.

"Quon is waiting," Lu Hom said when Ah Ching did not reply. "This way."

He followed Lu Hom down a long hallway, and then down a flight of steps. The smell of stale opium permeated the air, filtering down from the opium parlor two flights above them. He knew that Lu Hom liked opium, but his eyes showed that he was not now under its influence.

When they reached the bottom of the stone steps, they were facing a door, and Lu Hom said, "Inside."

Without waiting, Lu Hom turned and started back the way he came. Ah Ching turned the knob on the door and entered.

In Chinese he was Quon Loo Chin, but in San Francisco he was known as Loo Quon, head of the White Pigeon Tong, and he had held that position for as many years as the Chinese were in San Francisco.

"Ah Ching," Quon said, and Ah Ching approached him. Quon sat behind a small desk, upon which sat a small storm lamp and some burning incense. The desk had no legs, and Quon sat cross-legged on the floor. From his appearance, the man could have been anywhere from sixty to a hundred. His skin was old and creased like yellowed parchment. His hair, what little there was, was white and wispy, and this man who many feared could not have weighed more than a hundred pounds.

"You requested a meeting," the old man said.

"Yes," Ah Ching answered, looking at the old man's eyes, which leaked mucus.

"Then speak."

"It is about a man, Arthur Royce."

10

"A *lo fan*," Quon said, meaning a "white man."

"Yes."

"Speak, Ah Ching. I do not have time to waste."

"He is an important man in the politics of the *lo fan*," Ah Ching said, "but we did not know this when he came to our parlor to play."

"Fan-tan."

"Yes."

Quon closed his eyes, then opened them and said, "And you cheated him."

"He had much money," Ah Ching said.

"And you cheated him."

"Yes."

"He will not want it known that he was gambling in an illegal parlor," Quon said. "It will be taken care of."

The surprise was evident on Ah Ching's face.

"Did you expect to be punished?"

"Yes."

"And so you shall, when I decide on a fitting punishment."

"Yes."

"Go now, and send Lu Hom to me."

"Yes."

"Go!"

Ah Ching turned and quickly left the room, almost running in fear from the specter of the old man.

When he was out of the room and in the hall beyond, he did run, up the stairs and along the hall, until he reached a point where Lu Hom stood.

"He wants you," he told the little Chinaman, panting.

"You are most fortunate," Lu Hom said.

"Why?"

"You are fortunate that he did not want me while you were still with him." Lu Hom started down the steps, then turned and said, "You will let yourself out."

"The door—"

"—will be locked behind you. Go now, and hope that you do not see me again...soon."

11

Ah Ching made haste to leave, not only that place, but Ross Alley, fervently hoping that he would never see Hom Lu Sin again.

And knowing that this could not be so.

[1]

Tracker was in the Farrell House bar having fan-tan explained to him by Will Sullivan, when Deirdre Long came looking for him.

"Wait a minute," Tracker said, looking down at the peanuts Will had been using for his demonstration. "Run this by me one more time."

"Okay," Sullivan said, "these peanuts are brass coins. The dealer takes a random number of coins from a big bowl, places them on the table, and covers them with a metal cover, like the cover of a kitchen pot. Follow?"

"So far," Tracker said. "Go ahead."

"The players try to guess how many coins will be left when the amount of coins underneath the cover is divided by four."

"Since when can *you* divide by two, let alone four?" Tracker asked his bartender.

"Tracker, there you are," Deirdre said, coming toward them.

"In a minute, Dee," he told the lovely blond girl who was his partner in the Farrell House hotel. "Go ahead, Will."

"Well, that's it. After all the bets have been made,

the dealer removes the cover and with some kind of a skinny stick—"

"A wand," Deirdre broke in.

"Right, a wand," Sullivan said. "Using his wand, he spreads the coins out in four even groups until one, two, three, or none are left."

"So you bet on whether there's going to be one, two, three, or none left."

"Right."

Tracker looked at Deirdre, who said, "That's fan-tan."

"How do you know about fan-tan?" he asked her.

"My father taught me. If you guess right, you get paid four times the amount of your bet, unless you split your bet, in which case you get paid at two to one."

Tracker looked at both Will Sullivan and Deirdre, then shook his head and said, "I'll stick with poker. Give me another beer, Will."

"Sure, boss."

Tracker scooped up the "fan-tan" peanuts from the bar and asked Deirdre, "Were you looking for me when you came in here?"

"Why else would I come in here?" she asked.

"You're right," he said, "that was a silly question. What's up?"

"Duke wanted me to tell you that he made an appointment for you later on this evening."

"After dinner, I hope."

"Before."

"Great." Sullivan brought his beer, and he said, "Thanks, Will." To Deirdre he said, "Do you want a drink?"

"No, thank you."

"Is that all you came in here to tell me?"

"Yes. Duke didn't want you disappearing before knowing—as you've been known to do in the past." Then, remembering that many times when Tracker does "disappear" he spends the time with Will Sullivan's sister, Shana, Deirdre turned on her heels and walked away without another word.

"Boss," Sullivan said, "sooner or later you're gonna have to pick between Shana and Deirdre. Either that, or get killed by one of them."

14

"You're only half kidding, Will, but you may be right," Tracker told his friend. He tossed off the rest of the peanuts, washed them down with the beer, and said, "See you later, Will."

"Stay healthy."

Tracker stopped short, said, "I'll try," and then continued on.

He passed through the doorway that connected the saloon to the hotel and walked through the dining room into the lobby. From there he saw Deirdre walking stiff-backed up the steps to the second floor. It was only her stubbornness that kept him from freely enjoying, not only *her* charms, but those of the fiery-haired Shana Sullivan as well. Shana, the more uninhibited of the two, did not mind sharing him at all, but Deirdre did it against her better judgment.

For this reason, Deirdre and Shana were not exactly the best of friends, and the situation was not helped any by Shana's working in the hotel.

In fact, at that moment it was Shana who was behind the front desk, and Tracker went over to her.

"Your brother was just telling me about his new hobby," he said, by way of greeting.

"Fan-tan?" she asked, looking up. "Tracker, I wish he'd stay out of Chinatown."

"Don't tell me you're worried about that big lug, the former heavyweight champion of the Barbary Coast."

"Look, you take a lot of little Chinamen and you put them one on top of the other, and you know what you get?"

"A Chinese totem pole?"

"One big Chinaman!" she said, ignoring his remark.

"Shana, your brother can take care of himself."

"Yeah, maybe, but ever since he got involved with fan-tan, and white pigeon ticket, and—"

"Whoa, hold it," Tracker said, "back up a second. What the hell is white pigeon ticket?"

"He didn't tell you about that yet?"

"I just barely got the hang of fan-tan, so I guess he decided to take pity on me and skipped the, uh, pigeon—what?"

"White pigeon ticket," she said again. "I can't explain it to you now—it's a kind of lottery."

"All right, forget that for now."

"Tell that to Will!" she snapped. "Tracker, please, can't you talk to him? I'm afraid of what will happen if he keeps going to Chinatown to gamble."

He touched her arm and said, "All right, Shana, settle down. I'll talk to him first chance I get, okay?"

She smiled and said, "Thank you."

"Do you know where Duke is?"

"In the office, I think. He was going there a little while ago."

"Good. I'll see you later."

He took his hand from her arm and walked around the desk to the office in the back. She watched until he closed the office door behind him, wondering what it was about him that made her stomach flutter. She wished she knew where she stood with him. All she knew was that he seemed to split his time between her and Deirdre, but she had no idea what he did—or who with—when he was off on a job.

A prospective guest came in at that point and she was glad for the distraction, because thinking about Tracker almost always made her a little crazy.

[2]

Duke Farrell was, indeed, in the office, sitting behind one of the desks in the room. One of the first things Tracker had done when he decided that he would keep the hotel he had won in a poker game was to add another desk to the room, a larger one than the one Deirdre had been using. Now the small one was exclusively hers, while the large one was split between Tracker and Duke. Duke handled most of the business, as Tracker preferred to remain in the background.

When Tracker entered, Duke looked up and said, "There you are."

"Deirdre told me that you'd like me to stick around."

"Depends on whether you want to work or not," Duke said. "That's always your decision."

"Uh-huh," Tracker said, pulling a chair over and sitting down. "Anybody get here yet for the game?"

"Not yet, but they're really not due until later today and tomorrow. Have you decided whether or not you're going to play?"

"Not yet, but I don't think I want to be out of town during this game. There are going to be some pretty big names here."

17

"I know it."

Tracker leaned forward and asked, "Then why did you make an appointment for me to see someone?"

Duke stopped shuffling paper in order to give Tracker his full attention.

"The man who wants to see you lives in San Francisco, and has indicated that this is where the job would be. You wouldn't have to leave town."

"Open that bottom drawer," Tracker said.

"Which one?"

"The one on your left."

"There's nothing in there."

"Open it."

"All right, but I'm telling you, I don't keep anything in—" Duke continued to insist, but when he opened the drawer he stopped short.

"Take it out, Duke, and open it up," Tracker said. "I want to toast your having had a good idea."

Duke's face was half-hidden by the top of the desk as he said, "Have you ever known me to have a bad— No," he said, thinking again, "don't answer that."

He brought out a bottle of bourbon and two glasses and poured them full.

"Now put it back," Tracker said, accepting one of the glasses.

After Duke put it away, they sipped their bourbon and Tracker said, "Now I've got an idea."

"What?"

"When the guy comes to see you, I'll talk to him in here, instead of in my suite."

"Fine," Duke said without hesitation.

"And I'd like to know as soon as people arrive for the game," Tracker said. "You know, if things go well, we could have this game every year."

"Sure, just don't ever put the hotel in the pot."

"This hotel has changed hands that way enough times," Tracker assured his friend. He finished his drink and stood up, depositing the glass on the desk. "Clean that up and put it away for me, will you?"

"Sure."

Tracker started to leave, then turned and said, "And

if you're going to drink my booze now that you know it's there, make sure you replace the bottle."

"Don't worry," Duke said. "I know a good idea when I see one, remember?"

"Yeah," Tracker said, "I remember."

[3]

The man's name was Arthur Royce, and he was a United States senator. When he arrived at the hotel, Shana notified Duke, who took the senator into the office and dispatched Shana to find Tracker.

Tracker was in his room...with Deirdre.

"Oh, God!" Deirdre shouted. Tracker's head was trapped between her thighs, and waves of pleasure went surging through her as his tongue lashed at her clit again and again. "Oh, Jesus, please, Tracker, you're making me...please, put it in me now, please..."

Holding her thighs down tightly to the bed, Tracker continued further until she was unable even to put words together in a sentence, and then he raised himself over her and drove himself in to the hilt.

"Jesus," she said soundlessly. Wrapping her arms and legs around him, she held on while he drove into her, holding her buttocks easily in his large hands, squeezing her flesh every time he plowed into her. She was helpless in his arms and she loved it...until a few hours later, when she hated it—until the next time.

He bent his head so that he could suck on her pink

nipples, rolling them in his mouth. She sighed and
moaned and cried out until she lifted them both up off
the bed, and then he was emptying into her and both
of their worlds were centered in that small junction
where they were joined.

He was such a large man, but she never seemed
aware of his weight until he took it away from her and
was lying beside her, as he was now.

They waited a few moments until they had both
caught their breath, but before they could speak there
was a knock on the door.

Deirdre looked quickly at Tracker, who simply mo-
tioned her to keep silent.

"Yeah?" he called out.

"Tracker, it's Shana."

Deirdre made a face, and Tracker called out, "What
is it, Shana?"

There was a moment's hesitation, and then Shana
called back, "Duke wants you to come down to the office."

"Tell him I'll be right down."

Tracker started to sit up, but Deirdre stopped him
by putting both hands on his chest, and then she kissed
him.

"I've got to go," he told her.

"I know," she said, moving away so he could rise and
begin to dress. She watched him, enjoying the graceful
way he moved.

"How can you be so big without being clumsy?"

"If I was even the least bit clumsy," he answered,
"I'd have been dead a long time ago."

The last item he put on was his gunbelt.

"Even in San Francisco you wear that?" she asked.
"Why don't you wear a shoulder rig, like the other
gentlemen?"

"Don't let the suit fool you," he advised her. "I'm no
gentleman."

Of late Tracker had taken to wearing dark suits instead of his traditional western garb. Trying to keep a
low profile was hard enough for a man his size, without
having his clothing cause him to stand out, as well. The
navy Colt he wore, however, was the right size for his

21

hand, and to exchange it for a smaller model to be worn beneath his arm would not have been a wise choice.

"Do you think she's waiting outside the door?" Deirdre asked.

"Would you be?"

"Of course not."

"You're not all that different, you know," he told her.

"Of course we are."

"If you would give each other half a chance, you could become friends."

"Not as long as you're in the middle, Tracker."

Knowing that she was probably right, he said, "I'm going to be discussing business, Dee, so I don't think I'll be back soon."

"Don't worry," she said, reclining on the bed with her hands behind her head, pert breasts thrust out at him, "I have my own work to do."

It was hard to leave with her lying there like that, but Tracker had made a lifetime out of accomplishing difficult things, so he opened the door and left.

When he passed Shana, who was back behind the desk, she gave him a knowing wink and a smile. It was amazing to him how she did not seem to mind sharing him at all, while Deirdre hated it. Still, they were alike in several ways, and probably *could* have become friends if it weren't for him. Knowing that, however, wouldn't make it any easier for him to make a choice between them, should the time ever come—which he doubted. He just wasn't the one-woman kind.

Upon entering the office he saw Duke seated behind the desk and a second man sitting in front of it. The other man turned to look over his shoulder as Tracker entered, and then stood up.

"Mr. Royce, this is Tracker," Duke said, also standing up. He moved out from behind the desk, because he knew Tracker would want to sit there.

Tracker crossed the room and shook hands with "Mister" Royce.

"A pleasure to meet you, sir," Royce said.

"Only if I can help you, I'm sure," Tracker replied.

"Uh, yes, well, I hope that you can."

"Duke," Tracker said, "now that I've met Mr. Royce..."

22

"I have things to do," Duke said as Tracker trailed off, "so I'll leave you two gentlemen alone."

Tracker waited until Duke left, then moved behind the desk and sat down. Royce was a big man, going to fat, and he dropped his corpulence heavily into his chair with a sigh. His hair was brown and sparse, even though he was only in his midforties, and he wore a bushy mustache, as if to make up for it.

"It's your time, Mr. Royce, so I suggest you do the talking."

"Yes, of course," Royce said, dry-washing his hands nervously. Tracker allowed the man to take his time.

"I think, first, that we should establish who I am," Royce finally said. "I am Arthur Royce, United States senator—"

"That may matter to you, Senator, but it doesn't matter to me," Tracker said, interrupting. "All I care about is what you want me to do and how much you're willing to pay."

"Fair enough," Senator Royce said after a moment's hesitation. "However, the fact that I am a senator will make it clear to you why I have come to you instead of having this matter taken care of through other, eh, channels."

"I understand," Tracker said. "You don't need any bad publicity."

"Precisely."

"I don't go around publicizing my client list in the newspaper, Senator. Can we get on with the business at hand, please?"

"Certainly. I have a particular vice, Mr. Tracker—"

"Just Tracker."

"As you wish... Tracker. It's a vice that a politician would be much better off without."

"Women or gambling?"

"Gambling, I'm afraid."

"Somebody is holding your markers?"

Royce frowned and said, "This is not something that is very new to you, I see. I suppose that should give me a measure of confidence in you." He paused to reflect on that, and then brightened and said, "Yes, I believe it rather does."

"Which gambling house were you in?" Tracker asked.

"Nothing you'd find in Portsmouth Square, I'm afraid."

Tracker thought that over a moment, then said, "Chinatown?"

"I'm afraid so."

"Fan-tan, white pigeon—" Tracker began, exhausting his knowledge of the games played in Chinatown.

"Yes, precisely," Royce said. "More and more, Tracker, I'm becoming convinced that I've picked the right man for the job."

"Now let's see if I pick the job."

"I suppose that means we must discuss your fee," the senator said. "I lost quite a large amount of cash, I'll admit, but that is of no consequence when measured against the amount of damage that would be done to my career if those markers should surface, or find their way into the hands of my enemies."

"Your career means very little to me, Mr. Royce. I have no interest in politics. I want to know how much I'll make if I recover those markers for you."

"I will pay you the full worth of the markers."

"Fine," Tracker said, "and how much is that?"

"Twenty thousand dollars."

Not a bad figure, Tracker thought, and he didn't have to leave town to make it.

"All right, Mr. Royce, I'll accept the job."

"Good!"

"Did you lose all of the money in one place?"

"Yes, a gambling hall on Dupont Street, run by a man called Ah Ching. Do you know Chinatown?"

"Actually, no, I don't, but I'm sure I can get someone to take me around. That's not a problem. How will I get in touch with you when I've recovered the markers?"

"You won't be able to contact me directly," Royce said. "I've taken a big enough chance just coming here. I will give you the address of my assistant, and you will get in touch with him."

"I won't turn the markers over to anyone but you," Tracker said, "and I expect to be paid at that time."

"Of course," Royce said, getting up to leave.

"Tell me something, Senator," Tracker said.

"What?"

"If you're so worried about your career, how did you allow yourself to get in so deep that you had to sign those markers?"

"I'm the first to admit that gambling is an illness, Tracker," Royce replied, "and that I have it."

"Seems to me you'd better get rid of it, then," Tracker said, "or else forget about politics."

"You may be right, Tracker," Royce said, "you may be right."

No money changed hands before the two men parted company. Tracker would reap no profit without results. That was the way he worked. It had been the way he'd worked as a bounty hunter, which was the only thing his former occupation and his present one had in common. The closest Tracker could come to naming his new profession was "recovery agent," which was as good a name as any.

Tracker opened the bottom drawer and took out the bottle and one of the glasses. Pouring himself a drink, he went over the conversation in his mind, and he was not convinced that the senator had been totally candid with him. Still, twenty thousand dollars was a lot of money, and Tracker did not think that he had been lied to, exactly. He simply felt that he had not been told everything.

Working under that assumption should enable him to avoid any major surprises.

There was a knock on the door and Duke entered without waiting for an invitation.

"Finished with your business?"

Tracker waved him in and took a second glass out of the drawer. Duke sat and accepted a drink from his friend.

"I'll be doing a little job for the senator," Tracker said, "but it shouldn't interfere with our poker game. Anyone arrive yet?"

Duke noticed the way Tracker had quickly skimmed over his "job," as usual, and didn't comment. Tracker never talked about his business with anyone, not even Duke, who was his closest—if not his only—friend.

"Poker Angie is here," Duke said, "and she's asking for you."

25

A funny kind of smile spread across Tracker's face, and he said, "It figures she'd be the first to arrive."

"I gave her the best suite in the place, aside from yours," Duke said. "It's on your floor, though—of course."

"Of course," Tracker said. He put away the bottle and stood up behind the desk.

"Far be it from me to give you advice about women—" Duke began.

"Nothing's ever stopped you before."

Duke went on, undaunted by the remark. "Keep Angie away from Shana and Deirdre."

"Deirdre, anyway," Tracker said. "Shana's no problem."

"Not when it comes to Deirdre," Duke said, "but Angie might be a whole different matter."

Tracker paused a moment, then circled the desk and started for the door.

"Who checked her in?"

"I did, but Shana was there and heard her ask for you."

Tracker put his hand on the doorknob and said again, "Shana won't be a problem."

As he left the room, Duke asked no one in particular, "Who is he trying to convince?"

[4]

Angela Harpe had earned the name "Poker Angie" by
cutting a wide swathe through poker tables across the
country since she was eighteen years old. Although
many of her earlier days were spent toiling away in a
somewhat older profession, she had nevertheless continued to sharpen her skills—including "reading" men,
which came in handy at a poker table.

Tracker had crossed paths with Angie more than a
few times over the years, with sparks inevitably flying
as a result. At this point in their lives, they were old
friends, and Tracker felt a genuine warmth building
up inside of him as he ascended the stairs and approached her room. He hadn't seen her for almost three
years.

When she opened the door in answer to his knock,
they stood and examined each other critically.

"You don't look bad for an old man," she finally said,
well aware that they were almost the exact same age—
and that, in fact, it was she who was four months older.

He was pleased to see that she had not changed much
since he'd last seen her—hell, since they'd met. Her
hair was still as black as a raven's wing and piled atop

27

her head, her breasts were still full, with no hint of sag. Her wide brown eyes showed some wrinkles in the corners, but that did little to dim their luster. She was as lovely as he remembered, which he always thought impossible.

"I didn't think anyone could be as beautiful as I remembered you," he said to her, "but even my memory can't do you justice."

She took hold of his arms and drew him into the room with her, saying, "You always were an eloquent bastard when you were trying to talk a girl into bed."

"How much talking do you need?"

"Shut the door and find out," she invited. He turned to shut it, and when he turned back she was already half out of her dress.

He watched with pleasure as she undressed, and was pleased to see that, even unfettered, her breasts had very little sag to them. They were still firm and proud, with dark brown nipples that were already beginning to harden.

"Well?" she asked. "Is that all you intend to do, watch?"

He reached behind him to lock the door, then unbuckled his gunbelt and began to undress himself.

"God," she said when he was naked, "I'd almost forgotten what a huge bastard you are."

And she meant that in more ways than one.

As he moved to take her in his arms he was reminded of how tall she was. Tracker was six-four, and Angie was still more than an armful for him, probably the biggest woman he'd ever been with.

He covered her mouth with his, and she immediately went to work with her skillful tongue and lips, while her hands were between them, drawing his erection even fuller. He reached behind her to grasp her buttocks and pull her tightly against him, enjoying the way her hardened nipples rubbed his chest.

"Let's stop wasting time and get to the bed," she suggested eagerly, and backed toward the bed, pulling him by his erect cock.

Together they fell heavily to the bed and began to reacquaint themselves with each other's bodies. He tongued and bit her nipples while his fingers slid into

28

the slick wetness between her legs, starting a fire there that she hadn't felt since the last time they had been together.

When she couldn't stand being passive any longer, she moved herself down on the bed and positioned herself between his legs. Avidly she began to kiss his balls and cock, and he tangled his fingers in her hair. When she allowed the head of his cock to slide between her lips, he gasped, and he continued to groan as her tongue played him skillfully, as if he were a musical instrument. He was too large for any woman to take him completely into her mouth, but Angie took more than any other woman he'd ever known. She began to suck on him in earnest, and he knew that she would not release him until she had emptied him completely. She caressed his balls lovingly as she increased her suction, and finally he began to spurt into her mouth powerfully as she almost forcibly yanked his orgasm from him.

Without any exchange of words, they switched positions and he buried his nose and mouth in the dark, bushy tangle of hair that surrounded her fragrant nest. He lapped at her moistness, then darted his tongue inside of her, causing her to jerk her hips off the bed. He moved to her clit and began to manipulate it skillfully with tongue and lips, and as she approached her orgasm she began to plead, "Suck it, ooh, suck it hard, you bastard, suck on it..."

When he knew she was about to peak, he abandoned the area and began to run his tongue over her soft, smooth nether lips as her fists pounded the bed in frustration.

"You sonofabitch!" she hissed passionately. "You know I hate that. Make me come, you bastard!"

With tongue and lips he again brought her to the brink, at which time she snapped, "Don't you dare leave me like this, Tracker!"

He rolled her tight little nub between his lips until finally her belly began to tremble, and then he began to suck on it furiously as she grasped his head and rode out the waves of pleasure that were wracking her body.

"Oh yes, damnit, yes," she moaned, "oh, Jesus Christ, yes, yes, oh yeahhhh..."

His cock was rock hard again by this time, and now

he raised himself above her and poked at her portal with the swollen head, teasing her again.

"Come on, come on," she said, "put it in, Tracker, fuck me, do it hard, damnit!"

Angie was a demanding woman. That was the one thing about her he had never forgotten. He rammed his huge cock into her and began to ride her hard, and she demanded more and more of him. She reached between them to cup his balls and squeeze them gently as he continued to pound away at her.

"Oh, God, you don't know how I've missed you, you big brute," she groaned into his ear, and he wasn't sure whether she was talking to him or to his rigid manhood. But in a few moments it didn't matter who was talking to what because he was firing a jetting stream of semen into her, and her muscles began to contract around him, pulling more from him, demanding more and getting it, until he was totally empty yet still twitching inside of her.

"Well?" she asked after they'd caught their breath.

He was still lying atop her, and he raised himself up, leaning his weight on his hands, and said, "Not bad...for an old lady!"

[5]

Tracker took Poker Angie to a restaurant in Portsmouth Square, preferring not to dine in his own hotel. What he was actually doing was avoiding any kind of confrontation with Deirdre or Shana over Angie Harpe.

Over dinner they caught up on the past three years, during which Angie hadn't done much of anything but travel and play poker.

"You, though," she said, "how did you get involved in the hotel business?"

"Poker," he said, "plain and simple."

"You won it?"

He shrugged and said, "Some people will back a hot hand with anything."

"Only your hand was hotter."

"That time."

"Are you going to play in this big game you're sponsoring?"

"I haven't decided that yet," he said. "Sponsoring," he repeated, savoring the word. "I'm a sponsor, huh? Maybe that's what I should do, just be a sponsor and let the rest of you lock horns over the poker table."

"Are you starting to feel like an entrepreneur now?"

31

"Oh, no," he said, "nothing so grand."

"You're certainly not still hunting men for bounty, are you?"

"Not for bounty, no," he said, and didn't elaborate.

Angie, used to Tracker's closemouthed ways, did not push the matter any further.

"Has anyone else arrived yet?" she asked.

"Not that I know of. You're the first."

"Who's coming?"

"We're not all that sure of exactly who will show up," Tracker replied. "If we have a big turnout, we'll split into two tables, or more."

"This could turn out to be more than just a poker game, then," she said. "It could be a tournament."

"I doubt it," Tracker said. "It's not as if Farrell House was an established gathering place for the elite of gamblers. It may take a few years for this thing to catch on."

"Is this going to be a regular thing, then?"

"It depends on how it goes, I guess."

"I'm curious," she said then. "Why is the hotel called Farrell House?"

"Not too many people know that I own it," he answered, "and I'd like to keep it that way. I've only let it be known that I'm using the hotel as a base."

"For what?" she asked, then held up her hand and said, "Strike that. I didn't ask that question. So Duke is fronting for you?"

"Right."

"Why tell me?"

"We're friends, aren't we?"

"Sure," she said, then added, "closer than most, at that."

Tracker smiled and ordered drinks from the waiter while he cleared the table.

"Who are the ladies in your life, Tracker?" Angie asked.

"Ladies?"

She gave him a look and said, "I've never known you to limit yourself to one woman. Even I never expected that . . . and I'm pretty special, right?"

"Very special," he said, raising his brandy glass to her.

"So, who are they?"

"I have a partner in the hotel."

"A woman?"

"Deirdre Long. Her father was Frenchie Longo."

"I met her!" Angie said. "Years ago."

"She's much older now."

"She must be, to command your attention."

"You'll meet her later."

"Are you equal partners?"

"I own fifty-one percent of the hotel."

"How does she feel about the game?"

"She is Frenchie Longo's daughter," Tracker said evasively.

"She does know about it, doesn't she?"

"She knows, Angie, she knows," Tracker said. Deirdre did know, although she wasn't all that happy about it. "You'll meet her later."

"Is she the only one?"

"Who else would there be?"

"What about the redhead on the front desk?"

"Shana?" he asked innocently.

Shaking her head, Angie said, "Same old Tracker. Don't worry. I don't intend to make any demands on you while I'm here. That will be your department. My door is always open."

"Not the wisest policy in the world, considering that you're staying in the big city now."

"I've been to big cities before, Tracker," Angie reminded him, and indeed she had. Big cities in other countries, as well, he remembered. Her poker playing had not only taken her cross-country, but cross continent, as well.

"I sometimes forget how well traveled you are," he said.

She made a face and said, "You make me sound like some sort of old road."

"Never that," he said. "If you were an old road, there would be a sign on you that said Caution."

"Or, in your case, Reserved."

"Ha," he said. "You're about as much a one-man woman as I am a one-woman man."

She sighed and said, "I guess you're right. If I could

33

ever be a one-man woman, though, we both know who that man would be."

"Compliment accepted," he said.

"But not reciprocated," she added. "You're a careful man, Tracker. Always careful never to step where the ground won't hold you, and never to say something that might come back later to haunt you."

"If you haunt me, it's only because you're so damned beautiful," he replied.

"Compliment accepted."

They finished their drinks and Tracker paid for dinner. When they returned to Farrell House they discovered that none of the other players had arrived yet, so Angie decided to turn in, reminding Tracker what she had said about her door always being unlocked.

He promised to remember.

[6]

"You want to do what?" Will Sullivan asked the following morning.

It was early, and Tracker had caught Will in the saloon with no customers around yet.

"I want to go to Chinatown with you," Tracker repeated, "next time you go."

Will frowned and said, "According to my little sister, you were going to try and talk some sense into me about going there. What happened?"

"I don't want to gamble, Will. I've got some business there and I need a guide, someone who knows their way around."

Will thought a moment, then said, "Well, I don't know the area all that well, but I guess I know it better than you do."

"Dupont Street?"

"I go to Sacramento Street mostly, but I can show you some of the gambling halls on Dupont Street. When do you want to go?"

"I told you, the next time you do."

"I was planning to go tonight."

"That's fine."

"Okay. Meet me here tonight when I get done."

"I'll be here," Tracker said, tapping the man's huge forearm. "Thanks, Will."

"Sure, just don't tell Shana."

"I'll handle Shana," Tracker said confidently.

Tracker left the saloon and walked back through the hotel, feeling somewhat less confident than he had appeared moments earlier. Will's sister, Shana Sullivan, was as fiery and volatile as her flaming red hair. It was one of the things that attracted Tracker to her, but it also made her unpredictable and, at times, more than a handful—even for hands as large as Tracker's.

She was behind the front desk as Tracker entered the lobby, and frantically waved him over when she spotted him.

"Morning, Shana."

"Have you had a chance to talk to Will yet about Chinatown?" she asked anxiously.

"Uh, as a matter of fact, Shana, I just finished talking to him about it."

"Were you able to talk some sense into him?"

"I think so, but I wouldn't expect miracles just yet," Tracker said. "Give me a little more time."

"I really appreciate this, Tracker," she said, putting her hand on his arm. "Maybe I can show you how much...later."

"Maybe," he said noncommittally.

"That is, if you're not too busy with your, uh, friend."

"Which friend?"

"I think I heard Duke call her Angie?"

"Poker Angie," Tracker said. "She's an old friend of mine, Shana."

"How old?"

He ticked his finger off the edge of her nose and said, "None of your business."

"Maybe," she said, and then a potential guest approached the desk and claimed her attention.

"I'll see you later," Tracker said, and instead of sticking around to check the register, he went to the office to ask Duke if any of the other players had arrived yet. He found the little man behind the desk and put the question to him.

"Luke Short checked in this morning," Duke said,

to Tracker's surprise. "Don't be surprised," Duke said, "be flattered. He said he heard it was going to be a good game."

"Anyone else?"

"Not yet, but Short said that he heard Bat Masterson was coming in for it."

That surprised Tracker even more. Short he knew, having met him on two occasions, but he had never really met Masterson, although he had been in San Francisco the last time Luke Short was.

"Bat Masterson, Luke Short, and Poker Angie," Tracker said. "That's a game right there."

Duke had a couple of ledger books open on the desk in front of him, and now he exploded, "God, have you seen the price of beef these days?"

"That's your department, Duke," Tracker reminded him. "Just let me know when we start to lose money."

"We haven't lost money since you won the place and let me run it for you," Duke said, "and if I can help it, we won't."

"That's fine," Tracker said. "Has Deirdre mentioned anything to you about the game?"

"Not to me," Duke said. "In fact, it seems to me she's been extra careful not to say anything about it."

"I've noticed that, too," Tracker said. "Well, as long as she's not fighting the idea, I guess that's all that matters."

"A little too late for that, I'd say," Duke said. "Besides, she doesn't seriously fight you on anything these days."

Tracker ignored the suggestion that was cloaked in that statement and said, "I'm going to have a late breakfast in the dining room."

"Enjoy it," Duke said. "This is my breakfast." He indicated a pot of coffee on the desk.

"You work too hard on those books," Tracker said.

"That's why we haven't lost any money," Duke pointed out.

Tracker couldn't argue with that, so he left Duke to his books and went to have his breakfast.

[7]

Lu Hom left Ross Alley with distaste for his assigned task, but he dared not voice, or even show, that distaste to his master, Loo Quon, the master of the White Pigeon Tong.

Lu Hom was to go to Dupont Street, to the gambling hall run by Ah Ching, to collect the markers left there by the "important" *lo fan* who had gambled there and lost a few nights earlier. It was foolish of Ah Ching to have allowed such an important white man into his gambling hall. The tong did not need that sort of trouble, especially with a major politician from the same state in which they ran their operations.

One thing they could not do, however, was ignore the debt. Just as they religiously paid their own debts, so did they expect others to do the same. So, Lu Hom must collect the markers and bring them back to Loo Quon for proper disposition.

Lu Hom smiled as he recalled his last words to Ah Ching. The man would certainly feel chilling fear as the tong hatchet man entered his establishment, and Lu Hom knew that he would play on that fear, causing it to build to an even higher pitch. He enjoyed it when men showed him fear, and enjoyed it even more when the man was Ah Ching, whom he despised.

When Lu Hom entered Dupont Street a path opened up before him as people shrank back from him. As much as the people in Chinatown feared Lu Hom, they feared him even more because he had the White Pigeon Tong behind him.

The diminutive but dangerous hatchet man walked with his chin high, feeling ten feet tall as the people cringed in doorways to avoid his path. As he reached the door of the building he wanted, he turned to cast a glance both ways, his face a mask, not reflecting the great satisfaction he was feeling from the reaction of the people.

He presented his back to the street and knocked on the locked door. A viewing slot opened and a pair of almond-shaped brown eyes appeared, widened, and then disappeared. Lu Hom knew that he did not need to identify himself. Everyone in Chinatown knew who he was.

The door opened a few moments later and he entered, knowing that the time had been taken to announce his arrival. The servant who admitted him stood with his head bowed, not daring to look into his eyes.

The room was large, filled with smoke—and with people. Fan-tan was the game that was most in evidence, and the din of chattering voices was offensive to his ears. As he started across the room toward the door to the back office, he was intercepted by Ah Ching's daughter, Anna Ching.

She was incredibly lovely, and even Lu Hom was susceptible to her beauty. She was taller than he, but that was no matter, since most women were. Her dark black hair hung to her shoulders, parted just off center to the left; and her lips were touched with pink, and glistened as if she had just wet them with her tongue. She was much fuller in figure than the average Chinese girl, which was something else that did not escape Lu Hom's eyes. There was no lust there, however, only admiration...and a touch of pride.

"Why are you here?" she demanded in Chinese.

"Do not speak to me in that tone, woman," he replied in the same language. "I have come to see the old man."

"To kill him?"

Lu Hom smiled tightly and said, "To see him. Step aside."

"I will tell him you are here."

He brushed past her, saying, "*I* will tell him that I am here."

He moved swiftly toward the office door, and although she rushed after him, she was not able to reach him before he opened it.

Ah Ching looked up from his desk in annoyance at the interruption, but when he saw Lu Hom, the look on his face turned to disgust and fear.

"You," he said simply.

"Old man," Lu Hom said, chuckling at the look on the other's face.

"You have no right," Anna Ching cried, trying to push past Lu Hom to stand between him and her father.

"You have come to—" Ah Ching said, but his voice failed him before he could finish the sentence.

Lu Hom approached the desk and the old man cringed back in his chair. Anna Ching had both of her hands wrapped around Lu Hom's left arm, but it was as if she were not even in the room.

Facing the older man across the desk, Lu Hom extended his right hand and said, "I have come for the markers."

"The markers," Ah Ching said, as if he did not understand. When realization dawned on him, he sat up straight and said, "The markers? You have come for the markers? That is all?"

"That is all," Lu Hom said, then added, "this time."

Ah Ching hurriedly removed the markers from his desk and handed them to the little tong hatchet man. Lu Hom accepted them, examined them, tucked them away, and then turned to face Anna Ching, whose eyes were flicking anxiously back and forth between the two men.

"I am the right hand of Loo Quon," he said quietly, "and Loo Quon *is* the tong. Do not presume to tell me what I have and do not have the right to do." He turned to Ah Ching and said, "What I said to you last time holds. Pray that you do not see me again."

He turned abruptly, brushed past Anna Ching with no pleasure in the contact, and left.

Anna approached her father, who was shaking from a combination of fear and relief.

"He is as mad as ever," she said.

"Yes," her father agreed, "and more dangerous than ever. I will pray that neither one of us ever sees him again, for it would mean our deaths."

Mark Roberts was Arthur Royce's assistant, which meant that whenever something had to be swept under the rug, it was Roberts's job to make sure it was a clean sweep.

As Roberts entered Royce's office, the senator demanded, "Where the hell have you been?"

"Out, taking care of some business."

"All night?"

Roberts's handsome face broke into a smile, and he said, "Some business takes longer than other business."

Royce shook his head, trying to hide his envy of the success his young assistant had with women. The only time Royce could find a willing young woman was when he was paying for one.

"Sit down. We've got things to talk about," he instructed Roberts.

"Like what?" Roberts asked, obeying.

"I hired that fella yesterday."

"Tracker? He took the job?"

"He did."

"I still don't like it," Roberts said. "I don't know that much about the man, but what I have been able to find out about him doesn't make him sound like the ideal patsy."

"What did you find out about him that we didn't know yesterday?"

"He used to be a bounty hunter—"

"We knew that much."

"Early last year he came to San Francisco and settled down in the Farrell House hotel off Portsmouth Square."

"I know where it is, Roberts," the senator said in annoyance. "I was there yesterday."

Roberts ignored Royce's annoyance and continued.

"He's left San Francisco from time to time since then,

probably on jobs each time, then comes back and stays at the hotel. There's some speculation about his actually owning a piece of the place, or else why would he suddenly decide to settle down in it and use it as a base?"

"Who cares? He took the job, and that's all I care about," Royce said.

"So what do you want me to do now?"

"What do I want you to do?" Royce asked. "I want you to go and get those fucking markers, that's what I want you to do."

"How do you suggest I do that?"

"The way you do everything, Roberts," Royce said. "Efficiently. Just do what you have to do to get those markers, okay?"

"Okay."

"And now that Tracker is on the payroll, use him if you have to," Royce added. "Just make sure that if you do something…distasteful…that it doesn't come back to us."

"That's why Tracker is there," Roberts said, standing up. "I'll get it done, Senator. Don't worry about a thing."

[8]

It was an extra quiet day for Tracker, and he found
himself itching for the trip to Chinatown that evening.
It had been a while since his return from Missouri following the business with Jesse James—and Zee
James—and he was anxious to get back to work. He
didn't mind, however, that he was going to be able to
do this particular job without leaving San Francisco.

When Will Sullivan finished up his shift behind the
bar that night, Tracker was right there waiting for him,
nursing a beer.

"What about dinner?" Will demanded.

"Don't worry about dinner," Tracker said. "We'll get
something on the way—or on the way back."

"Thanks a lot," Will said, rubbing his stomach.

"Besides," Tracker added, eyeing the ex-boxer's
growing paunch, "you've been putting on weight ever
since you retired for good."

"Oh, yeah? Well, I can still go a few rounds with you
and make you remember it," Will said.

"No argument. Let's go out that way," Tracker said,
indicating the batwing doors that led to the street.

"Avoiding Shana, huh?" Will asked, giving Tracker

43

a knowing look. "She's still after you to talk some sense into me?"

"Which I intend to do tonight," Tracker replied. "You're my guide tonight, Will, which means there won't be any time for gambling. Got it?"

"Not even one little game of fan-tan?"

Tracker's curiosity caused him to weaken at that moment, and he said, "Well, we'll see. Maybe just one."

When they reached Chinatown, Tracker said, "Walk me around a bit, Will; let me get the feel of the place."

As they walked along Sacramento Street, the two men attracted a lot of attention, because they were head and shoulders above all the other people, most of whom were Chinese. Both Tracker and Will were large men, but walking among these Chinese people, they felt as if they were giants.

"Makes you feel kind of funny, don't it?" Will said.

"It does that," Tracker admitted. "This is one crowd you and I couldn't get lost in."

And that was the only word that could have been used to define the people who filled the streets of Chinatown—a crowd. The streets were literally teeming with oriental men and women, all either going to or coming from somewhere.

"Where are all of these gambling halls?" Tracker asked.

"Behind some of these doors," Will said. "You've got to knock and be admitted, and if you're not recognized, or you don't have the name of someone who recommended you, you won't get in."

Tracker sniffed at the air and asked, "What's that funny smell?"

"Opium," Will answered. "They smoke it in pipes, and although the opium dens are just as hidden as the gambling dens, the odor still gets out into the street."

"Opium?" Tracker asked, looking at his friend. "How much do you know about that?"

"I don't know nothing about that, except what I hear," Will said. "I don't get involved with no drugs, Tracker. I was a fighter; I got too much pride in my body to fill it with drugs."

"Okay, Will, okay," Tracker said soothingly. "I was just asking."

"This is where I usually do my gambling," Will said, pointing to a door.

"Take me in."

"That's not where you want to go, though."

"I know, but how different can these places be? It'll give me some idea of what to expect."

"Okay," Will said, "I'll try to get you in."

Tracker followed Will to the door, which the ex-boxer banged on with his massive fist. A small eye slot opened to allow a pair of eyes to inspect them, and then closed. The door was opened by a small, elderly Chinese man, who pointed to Will and nodded.

"Wait here," Will told Tracker, and then stepped through the door, which closed behind him. Tracker waited a few moments, then the door opened and Will reappeared.

"Okay," he said, "come on in."

Tracker stepped in and the elderly Chinaman closed the door behind them.

"What happened?" he asked.

"I've been here a few times," Will said, "and I told them you were with me. It's been okayed."

"Let's go, then," Tracker said.

They followed the old man down a long hallway, past a stairway.

"What's up there?" Tracker asked.

"Can't you smell it?"

Tracker sniffed, and it was the same scent he had caught out in the street, only much stronger. Opium.

The Chinaman said something in Chinese, gesticulating wildly, and Will said, "I think he wants us to get away from the stairs."

"Well let's go, then, before he has a heart attack."

They followed the elderly man along the hallway until they reached a closed door, which he opened with a key. When he swung it open they were struck by the odors of stale smoke and sweating bodies.

"Jesus, it's hot in there," Tracker said, taking a step back.

"That's because that's where all the action is," Will said. "Come on, we'll find a fan-tan game."

Tracker followed Will into the room and was surprised at how many people there were, and at how loud it was. He couldn't remember ever having been in a saloon or gambling hall that was quite as noisy.

"These people are dead serious about their gambling," Will said over his shoulder.

"I can see that," Tracker said, as two Chinamen stood up from a table and began to fight.

Tracker knew better than to risk money on a game he knew little or nothing about, so when Will stopped at a fan-tan table, he simply watched his friend lose his money.

"I think that should be it, Will," Tracker said finally, ready to leave.

"Just one more," Will said without turning his head.

"Will, I want to get going," Tracker said, nudging his friend. "If Shana finds out about this, she'll kill us both."

Now Will looked over his shoulder and said, "I thought you said you could handle Shana."

"Under certain circumstances," Tracker amended.

"All right, just once more."

"No," Tracker said, grabbing Will's arm.

"Why not?"

"Because if you win, we'll never get out of here. Let's go; you can play one in the next place."

Will gave that some thought, then shrugged and said, "Okay."

They left that particular gambling hall, and Will led the way to Dupont Street, which was virtually identical to Sacramento Street in that it was teeming with Orientals and the air was filled with the scent of opium. The buildings were different, of course, but in essence they were the same.

"What now?" Will asked.

"We look for Ah Ching's," Tracker said. Then he looked at Will and asked, "You don't know where Ah Ching's is, do you?"

"I do my gambling on Sacramento Street," Will reminded him. "I wouldn't know an ah ching if I tripped over one."

"Then we'll have to ask."

Which turned out to be a lot less helpful than anticipated.

About an hour later Tracker said, "Either they don't understand English, or they don't want to."

"Even if they can't understand English," Will said, "they should be able to understand 'Ah Ching.'"

"Sometimes I forget that you're not as dumb as you seem," Tracker said, "but all that means is that they don't want to understand us."

"Or they don't want to tell us where Ah Ching's is. I wonder why?"

"You think it's something about the way we look?"

Will leaned against a wall and said, "What now?"

"I think maybe I should have picked out a Chinese guide instead of an Irish one," Tracker said. "Let's go home, Will."

"How about we stop back at Sacramento Street for one more—" Will began, but Tracker cut him short.

"I think while we walk home I'll have that talk with you that I promised Shana—the one about not gambling anymore."

"Not gambling in *Chinatown* anymore," Will corrected him.

"I'm glad you see it my way, Will," Tracker said, clapping his friend on his broad back.

[9]

It was late as they started back, and their progress did not go unnoticed. They were, in fact, being followed, for word had gotten around that two *lo fan* were looking for Ah Ching's gambling hall, and instructions to all were that the two seekers were not to find it under any circumstances.

That done, a new set of orders went out, which resulted in Tracker and Will's exodus being observed by more than one set of eyes.

As Tracker and Will turned into an alley that would lead them out of Chinatown, both men were brought up short by what they saw.

"Oh, shit," Will said.

"Yeah."

The alley ahead of them was totally devoid of movement or life of any kind, which was as shocking to them as if it had been littered with dead bodies.

"I ain't never seen this before in Chinatown," Will said in an awed whisper.

"I don't like this," Tracker said. "I think we'd better turn—"

At that moment something struck him a solid blow

in the small of the back and sent him reeling into the alley. Scant seconds later Will Sullivan staggered alongside of him and both men fell to the ground together.

"What—" Will started to say as they sat up, but he stopped short as both he and Tracker noticed that they were not alone in the alley, not by a long shot.

They couldn't make out faces, but they could make out shapes, and there were at least half a dozen surrounding them. Tracker was reminded of what Shana had said about taking a lot of Chinamen and piling them one on top of another.

"You seek Ah Ching's," one of them said.

Tracker put his hand to the small of his back, which ached, and said, "That's right."

"That is wrong," the voice said. Tracker squinted to try and pick out which shape was doing the talking, but he couldn't tell. "You do not seek Ah Ching's anymore. Understand?"

"Wait a minute—" Will began, but a man's foot came out and crashed into his chest, knocking him back.

"Hey—" Tracker said, and the same man's foot came out and stopped just short of his chest.

"You listen, please," the man said in accented English. "You look no more for Ah Ching's. Understand?"

"Tracker," Will said, pushing himself up to a seated position again, "there ain't but six of them, and we outweigh them all put together. What do you say?"

As an answer, Tracker grasped the foot that was scant inches from his chest, twisted and pushed back, and the foot's owner fell to the ground.

Will bellowed and sprang to his feet, fists flailing away, and Tracker followed his example. In seconds they were knee-deep in Chinamen, and the wading wasn't so easy.

Though much smaller, the Chinamen were fast, very fast, and as their fists and feet thudded into the two white men, there seemed to be many more than just six of them. Tracker realized that for every punch he was landing, he was being hit three or four times, and the blows were starting to tell on him.

It was time to admit that they were legitimately outnumbered and to pull out his gun.

49

He reached for his gun, felt his hand close around the butt, and drew it out of his holster; but before he could bring it into play, someone's foot struck his wrist and the weapon went flying into the darkness.

Not pausing to lament the loss of his gun, Tracker again began to lash out with his fists, but the blows coming the other way were coming too fast now, thudding into his chest, his belly, his legs. Next to him, Will Sullivan was suffering the same fate, even though he was attempting to bring all of his past boxing skills into the fight.

Tracker felt a blow on his cheek that sent him reeling to the ground. The blood was wet on his face as it flowed from his gashed skin, and then the kicks began. He rolled and rolled to try and avoid the blows, and in doing so he felt himself roll over something hard. More blows rained down on him as he reached beneath him to see what he was lying on.

It was his gun.

Grabbing hold of the weapon with his right hand, he raised it up and fired one shot blindly.

He pulled himself up against the wall and folded up his knees in an attempt to protect the gun as he cocked the hammer, preparing a second shot, this one well aimed; but before he could do so the six dark forms took off down the alley, and Tracker let them go, turning his attention to Will Sullivan.

"Will!" he called. He crawled along the hard ground toward his friend, who was lying much too still. "Will, are you all right?"

When he reached his friend he heard a moan, and as he touched his shoulder Will Sullivan turned over and mumbled, "Jesus, what the hell happened?"

"We got roped and branded by a bunch of Chinamen not even half our size."

"Shit," Sullivan said, wiping the back of his hand over his mouth, smearing his face with blood, "I won't tell nobody if you won't."

[10]

"What the hell happened to you two?" Duke Farrell demanded as Tracker and Will entered the office. They had come into the hotel through the back in order to avoid meeting Shana in the condition they were in.

"Don't ask," Tracker said. "Get that bottle of whiskey out of the bottom drawer."

Duke opened the bottom drawer, and Tracker caught the bottle in his big hand as his friend tossed it to him. He opened it and handed it to Will, who let the whiskey soothe the cuts on his lips as it burned its way down his throat.

"Give me some of that," Tracker said. He took the bottle from Will, spilled some whiskey on a kerchief, and held it to his bleeding cheek while he took a long swallow.

"Where did you guys come from?" Duke asked.

"A night on the town, Duke," Tracker said. "Just a night on the town."

Duke was about to say something else when there was a knock on the door.

"Yeah!" he called out.

"Duke, it's Shana," Will Sullivan's sister called back.

"Don't let her in!" Will hissed, waving his hands at Duke. Duke looked at Tracker and he nodded, indicating that the con man turned hotel man should listen to Shana's big brother.

"What is it, Shana?"

"There's a problem with a guest's bill. Can I come in?"

"No," Duke replied, "I'll come out. Wait for me at the desk, please."

"All right."

"What the hell is going on?" Duke demanded.

"We just don't want her to see her brother in this condition," Tracker said. "Go ahead and take care of her problem, and when you come back, bring another bottle."

"How about a doctor?"

Tracker looked at Will, who shook his head.

"Nothing here I can't handle," he said.

"No doctor," Tracker said. "Go on...and don't let Deirdre know we're here, either."

"All right, but I think I deserve some kind of an explanation," Duke complained.

"Bring back another bottle," Tracker said, "and then you'll deserve one."

When Duke left, Tracker took another pull on the bottle and handed it back to Will.

"How you doing, partner?" he asked the ex-boxer.

"I been hit harder."

"But not more often, I'll bet."

"They were fast, weren't they?"

"With their hands and their feet," Tracker said. "I've never seen anyone fight like that."

"Didn't hardly see it tonight, either."

"We sure felt it, though."

"I still can't believe it," Will said. "I still can't believe that even six Chinamen could do that to us."

"Did you see any of their faces?"

Will shook his head and said, "No, it was too dark."

"The voice sounded Chinese to you, didn't it?"

"It sure did," Will said, then he turned and said, "You think maybe they weren't Chinese?" in a hopeful voice.

"Whether they were or not, they were still half our size, Will," Tracker reminded him.

"Yeah," Will said glumly. He did some sucking on the bottle and handed it back to Tracker.

"Why?" Tracker said.

"Huh?"

"That alley was emptied out for us, Will; but why?"

"I don't know. I guess they were mad because we were trying to find Ah Ching's."

"Yeah, but why? You'd think Ah Ching would be glad to have more willing customers."

"Maybe it was Ah Ching's competitors who warned us off," Will suggested.

"Have you ever heard of that happening before?"

"I haven't, but I'm kind of new to Chinatown."

"Well then, maybe I should try and find out from someone who isn't so new."

"And speaks Chinese."

"Right."

"But who?"

"I don't know yet," Tracker said, standing up and stretching to relieve the ache in his back, "but I'll think of someone. I think I need to soak in a hot tub."

"So do I," Will said.

"Here, you take this," Tracker said, handing Will the bottle, "I've got one in my suite. Let's get out of here before Duke comes back. I don't feel like answering any questions tonight."

"I'm with you."

They left the office quickly and ducked into the back hallway without encountering anyone.

"Are you going to want me for another trip?" Will asked.

"You'd be willing after tonight?"

Sticking his chest out, Will said, "I was never one to duck a rematch in my time, Tracker."

Tracker grinned, then winced at the pain it caused his ripped cheek, and said, "I'll let you know, Will. Meanwhile, why don't you take tomorrow off. We'll get someone else to tend bar."

"No, no, that's okay," Will said. "I've taken worse beatings than this. I'll be here tomorrow."

"It's up to you. See how you feel in the morning. Good night, and thanks."

"Sure, boss."

Will used the back door to leave, and Tracker took the back stairs to the second floor.

In his suite he took out a bottle of whiskey and carried it with him, sipping it while he filled his tub with hot water. He settled into the water, still with the bottle in hand, and let the heat bake away his aches. The wound on his cheek had crusted over and stopped bleeding, and he left it that way rather than wash it out and risk opening it again.

When he started to doze off he got out of the tub to avoid drowning. He finished off the bottle and dropped himself into bed. Before falling asleep he remembered what Will had said as he left, and decided that the same was true for him, as well.

There would definitely be a rematch.

[11]

Tracker awoke the next morning with sore ribs and once again sought the healing powers of a hot bath. He was getting dressed when there was a knock on the door.

"Who is it?"

"Duke."

Tracker let him in, and the little man faced him with his hands belligerently planted on his hips.

"You disappeared last night before I could get an explanation," he said accusingly.

"I was tired, and I needed a hot bath."

"What about this morning?"

"No thanks, I just had another hot bath."

"You're not going to explain, are you?"

"Do I ever?"

Duke opened his mouth to answer, then closed it as he realized the uselessness of arguing.

"Well, you left before I could tell you that Bat Masterson and two other players arrived last night."

"Who are the other two?"

"Fred Doyle and Diamond Jack Hawkins."

"That's a nice quintet," Tracker said, "but the game is scheduled to start tonight. I hope we get a few more."

"I'm sure we will. Are you going to be around tonight for the start of the game?"

"I plan to," Tracker said, then added, "but if I'm not, you can get it under way."

"Does your condition have something to do with your new job?" Duke asked, then he said, "Never mind, that's a dumb question. All right, I'll mind my own business."

"That's good, Duke. Listen—"

"Yeah?"

"Do you know anyone who speaks Chinese?"

[12]

When Tracker went downstairs for breakfast, he checked the saloon to see if Will had arrived. He had, and was behind the bar, getting it set up for the day's business.

"Decided to come in, I see," Tracker said, approaching his friend.

"Good morning to you, too," Will said. "How do you feel?"

"My back aches, and a couple of my ribs."

"That cheek looks ugly."

"Yeah," Tracker agreed. The mirror behind the bar reflected Tracker's condition, showing his cheek to be crusted over and black-and-blue.

"Anyone ask about it yet?" Will asked.

"I haven't seen Shana or Deirdre yet, but I'm sure I can give them an explanation they'll accept."

"I haven't seen Shana either, but at least I don't have too many marks that show, except for a split lip."

"Just tell her you got into a fight," Tracker suggested. "I think she'd buy that."

"Sure," Will said, "I'll tell her I fought with you—about her honor."

"Tell her you fought with a woman," Tracker said. "She'll probably believe that even more."

Will grinned and said, "She'll say, 'One of *those* women.' That'll get me in more trouble than Chinatown."

"Figure something out," Tracker said. "I'll see you later."

"Right."

Tracker went back into the hotel dining room and spotted Luke Short and Bat Masterson seated at a table, waiting for their breakfast. He was debating whether or not to join them when Short looked up, saw him, and waved him over.

"Tracker, how are you?" Short asked when Tracker reached the table. "Bat, you remember Tracker, don't you?"

"Of course," Bat Masterson said. Masterson was a handsome man sporting a carefully trimmed mustache, and looked as if he was barely thirty. "The last time I saw you, you were in the ring, dodging fists and bullets."

"You helped me out, and I don't think I ever got a chance to say thanks," Tracker said. "Why don't you gentlemen let me buy you breakfast?"

"Will you join us?" Short asked.

"Why not?" Tracker said, sitting down.

A waiter came over and took Tracker's order, and he informed the man that the entire meal was to be charged to him.

"You look as if you've been ducking fists," Masterson said, "only not as successfully."

"Oh, this," Tracker said, touching his cheek. "Walked into a door, if you can believe that."

"If you want us to, we can," Luke Short said, exchanging amused glances with Bat Masterson.

Tracker didn't know exactly what they were thinking, but he decided simply to let them think it. It was better than trying to explain it away, and he had enough people to do that with already.

The conversation during breakfast consisted of current events, gambling, and women, not necessarily in that order. When Luke Short asked Tracker who else was in town for the game, Tracker rattled off the other three names, starting with Poker Angie.

"I've heard of her," Bat Masterson said, "but I've never had the pleasure of meeting her."

"I did, once," Short said, "and never having met her is your loss, Bat."

"That good, eh?"

Short nodded and said, "That good—and she's a good poker player, as well."

"One of the best," Tracker said.

"You've met her before?" Short asked.

"Oh yes, we're old friends," Tracker replied.

Short and Masterson exchanged glances again, and again Tracker did not elaborate.

"Have either of you ever played with Doyle or Hawkins?" Tracker asked.

"I haven't," Masterson said.

"I've played with Diamond Jack," Short said, "but not Doyle. He has quite a reputation for such a young man. He's even younger than you, Bat."

"We'll have to make sure his wet nurse is nearby," Bat Masterson retorted.

"Well, I've got to get going," Tracker said. "It was nice seeing you fellas again."

"Hey, whoa," Short said. "One more question, big man."

"Okay, shoot."

"Will you be playing in the game?"

"To tell you the truth, I haven't really decided yet, Luke," Tracker answered. "I guess we'll all find out tonight."

"We'll look forward to it," Masterson said.

"Oh, now I've got a question for you fellas."

"Fire away," Short said.

"How would the two of you feel about a rule that says leave your guns at the door when you enter the game?" It was an idea that had just occurred to him. Tempers had been known to flair at poker games.

Both men gave Tracker glances that could best be described as dubious.

"Ask a silly question," Tracker said. "Have a nice day, gents."

[13]

When Tracker got to the lobby he noticed that Shana was behind the desk. She had not been there the first time he had passed through. When she called out to him, his face was turned so that his injured cheek was hidden from her, and as he approached the desk she said, "There's a man waiting for you— What happened?"

"There's a man waiting for me where?" he asked.

"Uh, he's in the office," she said, still eyeing the gash on his cheek. "Duke put him in there."

"Who is he?"

"He said something about being someone's assistant," she said, studying his face. "Are you going to tell me—"

"I'd better go and see him."

"You're not going to tell me," she said in a resigned tone.

"We'll talk later, Shana," he said. "Thanks."

He went to the office, confident that he would find Arthur Royce's assistant, Mark Roberts. The question was why? It was too soon for him to be asking after results.

60

As he entered he surprised Roberts, who looked as if he had been bent over the desk. Now the man straightened and turned to face Tracker, an ingratiating smile on his face. He was young, in his early thirties, and tall—though not as tall as Tracker—and probably what women would call handsome. Tracker disliked him on sight.

"Mr. Roberts?" he asked.

"Tracker, isn't it?" Roberts asked, extending his hand.

"That's right."

Tracker shook the man's hand and then settled himself behind the desk.

"Can I get you a drink?"

"Sure," Roberts said. "Whatever you've got is fine."

Tracker took the bottle from the bottom drawer, broke the seal, and poured out two glasses.

"Is Royce looking for results already?" he asked, handing one glass to Roberts.

"Oh, no, that's not why I'm here," Roberts said, adding, "although from the look of your face, I'd say you were working rather hard to achieve results."

"This?" Tracker said, touching his cheek. "Walked into a door."

"I'm sure," Roberts said. "No, I'm merely here to meet you. I've got instructions to cooperate with you in any way I can, so I thought it would be wise for us to meet face to face."

"I see."

Roberts waited, as if expecting more to come, and when it didn't he groped for something to say. He wasn't ready to leave yet.

"Ah, I hope you don't mind, but I've done some checking into your past."

"Oh? Find anything I should be ashamed of?"

"That's hardly for me to say," Roberts answered, laughing shortly.

"Then why check?"

"I certainly had no intention of passing judgment," the man said, "although you do seem to have had some violent periods in your past."

"And you haven't?"

"Of course not."

61

"I thought so," Tracker said, and he was a hairs-breadth from a sneer when he said it.

Suddenly, Roberts was ready to leave.

"Yes, well, thanks for the drink," he said, standing up. "It was a pleasure to meet you. Don't hesitate to call on me if I can be of any assistance."

"If I come upon a nonviolent situation, you'll be the first to know."

Roberts's jaw tightened and he left, furious with himself because Tracker had been able to intimidate him just sitting behind a desk.

Using the big man was going to be a pleasure.

After the "assistant" left, Tracker poured himself another drink and thought about the man. He didn't know all that much about politics and politicians. Did they all have assistants, and if so, were they all like Roberts? He doubted that the man had ever done anything more violent than stepping on an insect, yet he was sure that the man was good at whatever he did.

Capping the bottle, he returned it to the bottom drawer, then swirled what was left of the whiskey in his glass. Mark Roberts had not come down there to Farrell House simply to meet Tracker.

A man like Tracker knew when he was being felt out, and that's what Mark Roberts had been doing, feeling him out.

That was what you did when you came up against an opponent you didn't know.

The only problem with that was Roberts worked for Royce, and Royce and Tracker weren't opponents.

At least, they weren't supposed to be.

[14]

Tracker knew that encountering Deirdre was inevitable. He also knew that she would not give up as easily as Shana had concerning the condition of his face, so when she walked into the office he readied himself for a barrage of questions.

"I was looking for Duke," she said, closing the door behind her. "There's a problem in the kitchen—" She stopped short when she saw his face. "What happened to you?"

"I walked into a door," he said, figuring *somebody* had to believe it.

"Don't try to con me, Tracker," she said, coming around the desk to inspect his face. She touched the edges of the gash with cool fingertips.

"You haven't even seen a doctor," she accused.

"Not necessary."

"Sure, tough guy," she said. She pressed on the wound and he flinched and grabbed her wrist. "Tough guy," she said again.

"Dee—"

"How did it happen?"

"Uh, Dee—"

63

"Wait a minute," she said. "Before you try a song and dance on me, let me say something."

He couldn't decide whether she was more beautiful when she was in the throes of passion or anger, but it was damned close between the two.

"All right, Dee, talk," he said, sitting back and crossing his arms over his chest. He liked to watch her when her eyes were flashing.

"You think it's funny, the way I feel about you, but it's not," she said.

"Wait a minute—"

"I'm talking!" she snapped, and he shut up. "This has nothing to do with my feelings, though. I have a free choice in that, but there's something I don't have a free choice in, and that's our partnership in this hotel. We're partners, Tracker, and what happens to you has an effect on this hotel. Don't interrupt!" she said, and he subsided again. He'd just have to wait until she ran out of steam.

"I haven't said anything about your poker game, although we're still battling over your wanting to turn this hotel into a gambling hall."

Actually, all he wanted to do was put in a few faro tables, just to give the big hotels on Portsmouth Square a run for their money, but he didn't mention that.

"This is different. You're my partner, damnit, and I want to know what happened to you!"

"Can I talk now?"

"Go ahead."

He stood up, walked around the desk, and took her by the shoulders.

"Tracker—"

He shut her up by kissing her. She resisted at first, but gradually her lips softened, her mouth weakened, and he was able to slide his tongue in. When he released her she was gasping for breath, and her eyes were slightly glassy.

"Damn you," she whispered. "Damn you, Tracker, you've got to prove who's boss, right?"

"Honey," he said, touching her face, "I know I'm not your boss. No man could ever be your boss."

He kissed her again, and her arms went around his neck. Her body strained against his, and if there had been a couch in the room, they probably would have ended up using it.

Abruptly, then, she put her hands against his chest and pushed, putting an arm's length between them.

"Don't think this gets you off the hook, Tracker," she said. "What happened to your face?"

"I got in a fight," he said.

"Over what?"

"I'm working, Dee."

"Here, in San Francisco?"

He released her shoulders and said, "That's right."

"And I've got to be satisfied with that, right? You got into a fight?"

"That's what happened," he said. "The why of it doesn't concern you—as a partner."

She recoiled from his words as if he'd slapped her.

"No, I suppose it doesn't," she said. "I've got to find Duke. There's a problem in the kitchen."

"Dee, maybe I can help—"

"No, that's all right," she said. "You're working; you've got better things to worry about than problems in the kitchen. I'll find Duke. He'll handle it."

"Sure."

Tracker allowed himself to wonder briefly if maybe he shouldn't start to get involved in running the hotel, but he put the decision off for another time. He had enough to handle right now, what with the game and the Chinatown thing. He didn't need to muddy his brain up with other matters.

Still, he couldn't help but think about the look on Deirdre's face when he told her that how he'd gotten hurt was none of her business. He'd make it up to her later . . . if she'd let him.

[15]

When Tracker entered his suite he found company waiting for him.

"My door was open last night, but you didn't come," Poker Angie said, "so I thought I'd come to your room."

"My door wasn't open," he said.

"That never stopped me before," she said.

He smiled and walked over to his bed, where she was lying beneath the covers. It was plain that she wasn't wearing anything but skin.

"Now, what would you have done if I hadn't come back here at all today?"

"I would have taken a nap so I'd be well rested for the game tonight."

"And now?"

"Now," she said, throwing back the covers, "I'll nap afterward."

He undressed, and she drew him into the bed with her and covered him with her nakedness.

"I missed you, you big bastard, and the other night just made me want you even more."

"I'm here to cater to your wants, Angie," he said.

"I want this," she said, and grasped his huge member in her hand.

She slid down until she was able to lave the swollen head with her tongue, and then drew as much of his rod as she could into her mouth.

"Christ, Angie," he said as she sucked at him furiously. His hips began to twitch almost uncontrollably, and when the time came a torrent of semen rushed from him into her mouth, which she swallowed with relish.

"Now me, now me," she said anxiously, lying on her back.

"You're shameless," he said, reversing his position.

She laughed throatily and said, "I know. Come on, Tracker, make me scream."

He buried his face in her bush and worked her with his tongue and lips until she did just that, although she did manage to muffle it with a pillow. By that time, his cock was at full attention again, and he climbed aboard and drove it into her.

"Yes, that's it," she exorted, "give it to me, give it to me good, you sonofabitch, just like I'm going to give it to those bastards at the game tonight..."

Tracker failed to understand the correlation between what he was doing and what she would be doing that evening, but he gave her what she wanted...not to mention what he wanted, as well.

"Oh, yes, that's it," she moaned, "that's it, please, just like that..."

As he fired into her he felt her nails rake at his back, but seconds later he was barely aware of it as the intense pleasure overcame him.

"Oh, yes," she said as he slid off of her to lie next to her.

"Now you've got another reason to take a nap," he said.

"And so do you."

"Oh, no," he said, sitting up and swinging his legs to the floor, "I can't. I've got things to do."

"Oh," she said, and he felt her hand touch his back. "What's wrong?"

"I've marked you," she said, tracing the lines of two

67

scratches, one deeper than the other. "I hope your other women don't mind."

"Don't worry," he said, starting to dress. "If they do, I'll just tell them where I got them, and they can take it up with you."

"Oh, thanks."

She watched him get dressed, enjoying the grace with which he moved, and then she said, "Do you mind if I just nap here instead of going back to my room?"

"Be my guest."

"Thank you." She stretched her body as much as she could, flattening her large breasts as she did so, and asked, "Are you sure you can't stay?"

He looked down at her, then ran his finger from her navel up to her right nipple, which he squeezed, and said, "It's tempting."

"No sale, huh?" she asked, writhing from the pressure of his fingers on her nipple. "Ooh, that feels good."

"There's more where that came from," he promised, adding, "only later."

"Are you going to play tonight?" she asked as he strapped on his gun.

"You're the third person to ask me that today."

"Who were the other two?"

When he told her she said, "That's interesting. Who else is here to play?"

"Diamond Jack Hawkins and Fred Doyle."

"Doyle!" she said, and he thought she was going to spit.

"You know him?"

"Unfortunately," she said. "He thinks he's every woman's dream, but all he is, is a nightmare." She shook her head and said, "I don't want to talk about him. Anyone else?"

"That's what I'm going downstairs to check on now," he answered, "if I can ever get out of here."

She reached for him and rubbed his crotch through his pants. "Don't think I'm going to make that easy."

"You're not," he assured her, "but luckily I've got a will of iron."

"That's not all you've got that feels like iron," she said as she felt him respond to her touch.

68

He slapped her hand away and said, "Control yourself, woman. I'll see you later."

"At the game? You never answered my question."

"I'll tell you what I told the others," he said. "I'll decide about that later."

"I'll look forward to it."

"That's what the others said, too. I'm beginning to think I'd better sit this one out. Too many people are anxious for me to play."

"We all just know how good you really are, Tracker," she said.

"And I know how good you are, Angie," he said, "but we were talking about poker, weren't we?"

[16]

The first time Tracker had asked Duke if he knew anyone who spoke Chinese, he had been kidding. Now,
however, he thought that Duke might just be his best
bet to come up with someone who could legitimately
guide him through even the darkest recesses of Chinatown.

Recalling that Deirdre had been looking for Duke
regarding a problem in the kitchen, that was the first
place he checked.

Deirdre had been absolutely right about one thing.
Tracker had never concerned himself with the problems
of the kitchen. The only time he had ever been in there
was during the first week he was in town, when the
back wall of the hotel had been set on fire. He ate in
the dining room almost every night, and he knew the
waiters, but he did not know any of the kitchen staff.

When he got to the kitchen he found Duke talking
to a man in a chef's hat—and the man was Chinese!
Deirdre wasn't there, so he approached the two men
and spoke to Duke.

"Can I see you for a minute, Duke?"

"Huh? Oh, sure." To the cook he said, "One minute, Toy."

The cook nodded shortly and turned his attention to some boiling pots.

"Duke, this morning I asked you if you knew anyone who spoke Chinese. Remember?"

"Sure, but I thought you were kidding."

"I'm not kidding now," Tracker said. "I assume that fella speaks Chinese?"

"Toy? Yeah, he speaks Chinese."

"Does he know Chinatown?"

"You'll have to ask him."

"He doesn't know me, Duke. Ask him if he'd be willing to guide me through Chinatown. I need someone who knows the area and the language."

"Okay, I'll ask him."

Tracker watched as Duke approached the cook and engaged him in a short conversation. The chef bobbed his head from time to time, and then at one point shook it emphatically.

Duke came back to Tracker and asked, "He wants to know what you're looking for."

"I'm looking for a gambling hall run by a man named Ah Ching, and I'm looking for a way in."

"That's what I thought," Duke said. "I don't know what's going on, but he just told me that if you want him to lead you to Ah Ching's, you can forget it."

"Damn!" Tracker said. "What's going on? Is that part of town closed to whites all of a sudden? Don't they want our money?"

"I don't know the answer to that," Duke said, "but I do know that you're not looking for this Ah Ching's in order to gamble."

"No, I'm not," Tracker said. "See what you can find out from him, will you, Duke?"

"He wants to know if he's fired. What do I tell him?"

"Hell, no, he's not fired—but let him think he might be unless he comes up with some answers."

"I'll see what I can get out of him."

"Thanks. I'll be in my suite."

As he walked to the front desk Tracker realized that he had forgotten to ask Duke if any other players had arrived.

"Shana, can I see the register, please?"

"Sure," she said, pushing it over to him. "Looking for someone in particular?"

"A few someones," he said.

"Ladies?"

"I doubt it."

He went down the day's entries and found two other players who had registered: Art Frazer and Jim Ward. Both were professional gamblers of little reputation, but at least they'd fill a couple more chairs. The game was a decent size now, with five of the seven players of top quality—not counting Tracker himself, who still didn't know if he was going to play or not.

"Okay, thanks," he said, pushing the register back to Shana's side of the desk.

"Find what you were looking for?"

"Yep, two more players for the game."

"How many does that make?"

"Seven, not counting me."

"Oh? How many women?"

"Just one."

"Just your old friend, Miss Sharpe, huh?"

"That's it," he said, "just Poker Angie."

"I'd love to watch her play against all those men."

"Sorry, Shana, no spectators at this game."

"How about somebody to serve drinks?"

"Honey, you'd be too much of a distraction up there, and Angie would clean up."

She grinned at him and said, "Maybe she'd split the profits with me."

"Angie wouldn't split her profits with her mother."

"Nice lady."

"She is a nice lady, but she's a vicious poker player."

"How did it go with Will?"

"Uh, Will. I don't think he'll be going to Chinatown for a while, Shana."

"Just a while?"

"Shana, honey, he's got to start somewhere, right?"

"I guess you're right, Tracker," she said. "I really appreciate your help, but when am I going to get to show you?"

"I'm just as anxious as you are, Shana," he said.

"Sure," she said, "as soon as Poker Angie leaves town."

"Now, Shana—"

"Relax, Tracker," she said, wishing that she cared as little as she was pretending to. "I almost forgot. Somebody left a message here for you."

"Oh? Who?"

"I don't know, but all of a sudden there was an envelope on the desk with your name on it. Here." She took it from below the desk and handed it to him.

"Thanks."

He took a couple of steps away from the desk and opened the envelope. Inside was a handwritten note that gave him specific instructions on how to find the gambling hall in Chinatown run by a man named Ah Ching.

"Shana, are you sure you didn't see anyone just before you found this note?"

"No one," she said. "Why, is there a problem?"

"You haven't seen any Chinese in the lobby today?"

"Not even the cook."

"Okay. I'll be in my suite, if anyone needs me."

"Does that include me?"

He remembered leaving Angie naked in his bed and asked, "Can you leave the desk?"

"No."

"That includes you."

[17]

Tracker went back to his suite to wait for Duke, and read the note again. It was simply explicit directions to Ah Ching's. Not even a salutation.

And it was unsigned.

Where was it from—Chinatown? Or somewhere else?

There was a knock on the door and Tracker called out, "Come in." It wasn't until then that he remembered and realized that Angie had been there and now she was gone.

Duke walked in and said, "No luck. Toy won't say a word, even if it means his job. He's scared of something, Tracker."

"I had some luck, though," Tracker said, handing Duke the note. "Shana gave me this. She said somebody left it on the desk for me, but she didn't see who it was."

Duke read it and said, "This is what you need."

"Right, but who's it from? And why?"

"Somebody who doesn't like being scared, maybe?" Duke said. "They decided to help you out on the sly."

"Maybe."

"You collect that check in Chinatown?"

"Yeah."

"The job for the senator?"

"Right."

"I don't even have to ask what it's about now," Duke said, handing the note back. "What are you going to do?"

"Follow the instructions."

"Alone?"

Tracker remembered the battle he and Will were in the night before, and realized that one or both of them could easily have been killed.

"Yeah, alone."

"Let me come with you."

Now Tracker remembered another time, in another part of town, when Duke had gone with him on a job and it was hours before Tracker knew whether or not the little man had gotten away alive.

"No, Duke. The hotel is your business, this is mine," he said, tapping the note against his thumbnail.

Duke might have remembered the last time, too, because he didn't argue. He didn't have to. He'd made the offer, and that was enough for both of them.

"You going to miss the game?"

"I'll try not to, but I'd better not go until after dark."

"I'll make your apologies." Duke started for the door, then turned back. "Everybody knows that this is your game, but what do I tell them about the hotel?"

"The hotel is none of their business, Duke," Tracker said. "That's what you tell them. Why, has somebody been asking?"

"Hints, only," Duke said. "I'll handle it."

"Okay."

"Be careful tonight, okay?"

"Yes, mother. Get out of here."

Duke nodded and left. Tracker went over to the bed, which was still unmade, and sat on it. He could smell Poker Angie on the sheets, and her scent excited him. It was just like her to leave the bed a mess. Poker Angie was not the domestic type. Shana was the same way, while when Deirdre left she always left the bed neat, as if a maid had been in to take care of it.

Tracker took his mind off women and put it onto work. For once in his life, his size was a huge disadvantage to him. There was no way he could possibly blend into a crowd on the streets of Chinatown. No matter how hard he tried, they would see him coming.

They'd be ready for him, and that was not a comforting thought at all.

Tracker decided that his best bet was to try and alter his appearance, hoping that he would at least look different enough to fool someone who had seen him there last night. He traded in his dark suit for his more familiar trail clothes, then took the sweaty, battered Stetson he had been wearing when he first rode in to San Francisco and put it on so that it shaded his eyes. Looking at himself in the mirror, all he saw was the same old Tracker, but then, how did you really go about disguising a gent who stood six-four, weighed two-forty, and had blond hair to boot?

He strapped on his gun, then looked out the window. Nightfall wasn't all that far away, and he decided just to stay where he was and wait for it.

While he was waiting, he practiced walking small. Maybe that would help.

[18]

Duke broke open a fresh deck of cards and said, "Let's
get this game under way."

"I guess Tracker's not going to make it tonight?"
Luke Short asked.

"He might make it later on," Duke said. "That is, if
nobody minds him sitting into the game late."

"It's his game," Bat Masterson said, and the consen-
sus around the table was the same.

"Then if everyone's agreed," Duke said, "I'll start the
deal. Seven-card stud."

"Deal," Poker Angie said, and the game was on.

Tracker was playing a different kind of game, and
it was called "follow the directions and hope you're not
walking into something you can't handle."

Walking down the streets of Chinatown, he felt like
a stallion in a herd of mules. At least when Will had
been with him there'd been two of them, but now he
felt not only alone, but naked as well.

He followed the directions until they led him to Dupont Street, where he stopped and stepped into a doorway. If he was being followed by a white man, he'd be

easy to pick out, but why would they have to follow him if they had given him the directions in the first place? It wouldn't have made sense, but he stayed in that doorway anyway and kept his eye on the street for a good half hour.

It was dark, and there were very few streetlamps in Chinatown. Still, the streets were full of people, as if the street traffic around there never let up, day or night.

Unless someone wanted it to, like last night.

If they'd emptied the street once to jump him, they'd do it again, so as long as the street was full of people, he was relatively safe.

He slipped out of the doorway and into the flow of the traffic again. It was odd, but he always seemed to have enough elbow room around him even when the street was this crowded; and on top of that, everyone seemed to be making a concerted effort not to look at him. He didn't belong there, and he should have been getting lots of looks, but the word had obviously gone out on him—which made him feel even more naked.

Finally, he found the door mentioned in the directions, and he knocked on it. The eye slot opened and two Oriental eyes looked out at him. The owner of the eyes didn't speak, but just kept staring at him as if waiting for him to say something that would make them open the door.

"I've come to see Ah Ching," he said finally, hoping that would get him in.

The eyes didn't respond; they just kept staring holes in him. Maybe the person behind the door didn't understand English, but they certainly should have understood the name Ah Ching.

"Ah Ching," Tracker said again.

This time the eyes blinked, and then suddenly the eye slot shut tight. He waited to see if the door was going to be opened, and when it wasn't he pounded on the door again, and kept pounding until the slot opened again.

This time he stuck the barrel of his .45 through the slot and the eyes widened.

"I can pull this trigger faster than you can move, my friend," he said. "Unlock this door now."

He heard the lock slide back, and then he pushed on

the door, keeping the barrel of his gun where it was. When he had the door opened all the way, the owner of the eyes was pinned behind it. Quickly he holstered his gun and shut the door, so no one outside could see what was going on.

The man against the wall looked like most of the people he'd seen in the street. Very short, with almond-shaped eyes that were now wide with fright.

"Ah Ching," Tracker said.

The Chinaman bowed his head and, hands clasped in front of him, started off down the long hallway with Tracker right behind him. He kept his hand on the butt of his gun just in case he needed to get to it fast.

This hallway was similar to the one in the place he'd gone with Will, except that there was no stairway. When they reached the end of it his guide opened a door, and the din that streamed out was even worse than it had been in that other hall.

Tracker stepped through the door with the China-man and shut it behind him.

Gambling tables were laid out all across the large, smoke-filled room, which was packed with people, but what Tracker noticed right off was the girl.

She was tall for a Chinese, with long, coal-black hair that hung past her shoulders. As she approached he saw that her almond-shaped eyes were larger than he'd seen on other Oriental women, her nose was small, and her mouth was full lipped and gracefully curved. She was wearing a tight, high-necked dress, which showed off the fullness of her breasts and hips and accentuated the trimness of her waist.

She stopped a few feet from him, regarded him coolly, and asked in good English, "Can I help you?"

"Yes, I'm looking for a man named Ah Ching."

"Are you here to gamble?"

"No, I'm here to see Ah Ching."

She abandoned him for a moment and spoke to the small Chinaman who had led him to the room. The man replied, and then she spoke to him curtly, an obvious dismissal, and he left, careful not to come any closer to Tracker than a few feet.

"You forced your way in here," she said to Tracker.

"Yes."

"Why?"

"I'm getting tired of saying this," he said, "but I would like to see Ah Ching."

"Ah Ching is my father," she said. "He is also an old man who tires easily." She lifted her chin and went on. "He has retired for the night. If you have business with him, you may take it up with me."

"I don't think so Miss... Ching? Is that correct?" Oriental names baffled him.

"Yes, Anna Ching."

"I would very much like to see your father, Miss Ching. I was looking for him last night and was attacked and beaten up for it."

"How unfortunate."

"The word seems to have gone out about me in Chinatown. Haven't you heard it?"

"I have heard no word, as you put it."

"About a big white man?"

"About any man, white or otherwise."

"My name is Tracker—"

"That means nothing to me."

She was as cool as ice, and Tracker was intrigued by her, even though she was giving him a hard time.

"How about the name Royce, Arthur Royce?"

She shook her head.

"Look, Anna," he said, "I'm willing to bet that the door against that back wall leads to an office, and that you father is in that office. This is a gambling hall. Would you care to take me up on that bet?"

"We have enough tables here to accommodate any bet that you might like to make, Mr. Tracker."

"I'm sorry, ma'am, but I'm going to take a look behind that door."

"I can have you stopped."

"And this place would get wrecked in the process. You might even lose some customers because of it. Can you afford that?"

She thought that over a moment, then made a decision she obviously didn't like.

She folded her arms in front of her and said, "Follow me, please. I will take you to my father."

"Fine."

He followed her down the aisles between tables,

keeping his eyes on the way her shapely rump moved beneath her dress.

When she reached the door she turned to face him and said, "Please try not to excite him. He is not well."

"I'm not here to excite him, Miss Ching. I promise you."

Actually, Tracker didn't know what he was going to say to the man. He had been so intent on reaching him simply because someone had been trying to keep him from doing so. What could he possibly say about Arthur Royce's gambling markers that would cause the man to turn them over? They were legitimate gambling debts, after all.

"Let's go," he said.

She compressed her lips, then turned, knocked on the door and opened it.

"Father—" he heard her say, and then she stopped short as her breath caught in her throat.

"Let me by," he said, squeezing past her. She was standing with her hands over her mouth, staring at her father's desk. Tracker assumed that the man slumped over the desk was her father.

He rushed to the desk to examine the elderly man, then turned to her and said, "Shut the door." When she didn't move, he said, "Anna! Shut the door!"

She shut the door in one convulsive motion, then slowly approached the desk as Tracker picked up the man's head and shoulders and leaned him back in his chair.

"Is this your father?"

"Yes," she said. "Is he..."

"He's dead, Anna," Tracker said. "I'm sorry."

From the serene look on the man's face, and his advanced age, it would have been very easy to assume that he had died of a heart attack or some other natural ailment, except for one thing—the lower portion of his torso was soaked with blood from a knife wound.

"He's been stabbed," Tracker said.

"Stabbed," Anna said. "Why? By whom?"

"I don't know. I—" He was interrupted by an insistent knocking on the door, and he and the girl exchanged glances.

"See who it is," he instructed her.

81

She went to the door and opened it a crack, then stepped back to admit the Chinaman who had admitted Tracker. He spoke to her in rapid-fire Chinese, and then she turned to Tracker and translated.

"The police are outside."

"The police?" he said. "Did you call them?"

"No."

"Do you pay them?"

She paused, then said, "Yes."

"Are you up-to-date on your payments?"

"Of course."

"I don't like this," he said, getting a bad feeling.

"Why are they here?" she asked.

"I think they're supposed to find me here," Tracker said, "with your father's body."

"But you did not kill him."

"They're supposed to think I did," he explained.

"Why?"

"That's what I want to find out, but I won't be able to do that from jail."

"You will find out who killed my father?"

"I'll try."

She turned to the little man and spoke to him in Chinese, then said to Tracker, "Follow Poon. He will show you a back way out. Where do you live? I would like to talk to you tomorrow."

He told her where he lived and then asked, "Will you be all right here?"

"I can handle the police," she assured him.

"No, I mean—"

"I will be fine, Mr. Tracker. We will talk tomorrow."

Poon moved toward the rear of the room, touched a panel in the wall, and a portion of the wall opened inward.

"Go," Anna Ching said.

"Why are you helping me?" he asked.

"Because then you will help me," she explained. "I will keep you out of jail, and you will find out who killed my father. That is a deal, isn't it?"

Still cool, even with her father in the same room, dead. Anna Ching was an incredible girl.

"Yes, Anna," he said, "that's a deal."

[19]

Tracker followed Poon through a man-made tunnel that had obviously been dug years ago. Whatever purpose it had been used for then—probably smuggling of some kind—it made an effective escape hatch now.

As he followed his guide, he realized that even though he was getting out without having come into contact with the police, he was not yet out of trouble. Someone had set him up for this murder, and whoever it was would not leave his discovery to chance. Once they found out that he hadn't been caught, he had no doubt that the San Francisco police would receive a tip to look for him at the Farrell House hotel.

He needed an alibi and he thought he knew where to get it. All he had to do was beat the police back to the hotel.

When they came up against a brick wall, Poon passed him the torch to hold, then grasped a particular brick and pulled on it as hard as he could. Tracker was about to offer his help when the wall suddenly opened inward.

"Out," Poon said, stepping back and pointing.

"I can see that," Tracker replied. He handed Poon back the torch, then said, "Thanks."

"Out," Poon said again, and Tracker couldn't tell if he was just being shown the way, or kicked out.

He stepped through the doorway and found himself in a darkened alley behind the building. When the wall closed up behind him, he was quite alone in the empty alley, and he remembered what had happened the last time he and Will had been on an empty street.

The alley was open on either side, and he chose the side that would take him away from the front entrance to the hall—and the police.

He moved into the busy streets again, moving with the flow of traffic away from Ah Ching's. He had finally found the old man he was looking for, only he was too late. Did the man's murder have any connection with Royce's markers? Damn, he should have looked through the old man's desk, or asked his daughter to do it after the police left. If the markers were gone, then there wouldn't be any doubt but that his job was connected with Ah Ching's death.

In a hurry to get back to the hotel, Tracker quelled his distaste for cable cars and took one that would leave him off near Portsmouth Square. When he got off, he hurried through the square and beyond it, to Farrell House, and entered through the back.

He approached the front desk from behind, and his sudden appearance startled Shana.

"Oh, Tracker," she said. "You scared—"

"I need your help, Shana," he said quickly, cutting her off.

Her first impulse was to ask questions, but when she saw how serious he was, she simply said, "What do you want me to do?"

"If anyone asks—anyone—you haven't seen me since the poker game upstairs started."

"You haven't gone in or out," she said, wanting to get it right. "Are you supposed to be playing in the game?"

"I am playing in the game, honey, and I have been since it started. All right?"

"All right, Tracker," she said without hesitation. "Anything you say."

"That's my girl."

"I wish."

He patted her hand and then went up the stairs to the second floor, where the game was being held in a suite. He had a key, and he used it to let himself in.

"Well, look who's here," Luke Short called out, and all of the players turned their heads to look at him, including Duke, who was dealing the game.

"We were just about to take a break, gentlemen," Duke said. "I suggest we do so."

Everyone concurred and moved to the far side of the suite, where a self-service bar had been set up. Duke approached Tracker and said, "What happened?"

"In a little while we might get a visit from the police," Tracker said. "Just follow my lead when they start to question me."

"About what?"

"I'll explain that later."

"What about them?"

Tracker looked over at the other gamblers, who were helping themselves to what the bar had to offer.

"They'll go along," Tracker said finally. "If you do, and Angie does, and Short, the rest won't say different."

"I hope you're right."

"We'll find out soon enough," Tracker said. "Let's get me some chips. At least I can claim I've played these big-time gamblers even all night."

"That's about the size of it," Duke said as they walked to the table for chips. "These guys—and the lady—have been playing even just about all night."

"No problem," Tracker assured him. "Class will tell sure enough."

"That means Doyle should be the first one out of the game," Duke said. "He's the worst player in the bunch, and he's got no manners, to boot."

"Oh?"

"He's been digging at Angie all night, trying to rattle her, but he's been the one getting rattled."

"Angie's running true to form, I guess."

"Same old Angie," Duke said. He turned to the players and said, "All right, lady and gentlemen, let's get back to the business at hand."

Everyone was in favor of that, and the game started up again in earnest, with Tracker starting hot. He took

85

three of the first four hands he played, and Doyle started to grumble right away.

Tracker was sitting directly opposite Angie, but she was indeed running true to form, for when she looked into his eyes it was only to attempt to read his hand. There were none of those coy exchanges of looks between a man and a woman who have been to bed together. Sex was fun, but poker was business, and Angie was all business.

It wasn't more than a half hour later when there was a knock on the door and Deirdre entered.

"Yes, Dee?" Tracker asked, trying to affect the look of someone who had been staring at the spots on a deck of cards for hours.

"Uh, could I speak to you for a moment?"

"Sure."

"Outside."

"Excuse me," he said to the table full of people. "Keep on with the game. I'll be right back."

He got up and walked out into the hall with Deirdre.

"What is it?"

"There are some policemen here, looking for you."

"What for?"

"You'd know that better than I would, Tracker," she said angrily. "What have you been up to now?"

"Playing poker."

"No you haven't. I was up here—"

"Dee," he said, stopping her before she could go any further. "I've been up here all night playing poker. That's the way it is."

She stared at him for a few moments, then lowered her eyes and said, "I see. What do you want me to do?"

"I'll come down and talk to the police. Take them into the office."

"All right." She started down the hall, then turned and looked at him with a question in her eyes.

"It'll be all right, Dee. I promise."

She nodded, then continued down the hall.

Tracker went back inside only long enough to take Duke aside and tell him where he was going.

"Keep the game going."

"Right. Be careful."

"Always."

"Sure," Duke said. "That's how you got yourself into this mess—whatever this mess is."

"You'll find out."

Tracker went downstairs and Shana turned her head and nodded toward the office. He returned the nod, then strode into the office, where Deirdre waited with two men, one of whom wore a policeman's uniform.

"Gentlemen, this is Mr. Tracker. Tracker, this is Officer O'Donnell, and Chief Preston."

Chief of Police Ansel Preston looked at Tracker with professional curiosity. He was a tall man—not as tall as Tracker, but better than six foot—with silvery hair and a neatly groomed brush mustache. He appeared to be in his early fifties and was well dressed for a lawman. The payoffs from the Chinatown gambling halls were no doubt the reason.

"Mr. Tracker," Preston said, "we have a few questions we'd like you to answer."

"Sure, Chief," Tracker said. "Always glad to cooperate with the law."

"Really?" Preston said dubiously. "That was something I hadn't heard about you."

"What have you heard about me?"

"That you're a bounty hunter."

"Not true."

"You've never been a bounty hunter?" Preston demanded.

"I didn't say that, Chief," Tracker corrected the man. "I said I was not now a bounty hunter."

"I see. Well, I'd rather not get into an argument over semantics right now."

Tracker wasn't sure he knew what the man meant, so he simply said, "What can I do for you, then?"

"I'd like to know where you've been all night."

"Upstairs, playing poker."

"Would you mind if O'Donnell went upstairs and checked on that for me?"

"Why?"

"Would you mind?"

"Not as long as you tell me why while he's doing it."

"Agreed."

"Deirdre, why don't you take the officer upstairs."

"All right," she said, although it was obvious she would rather have stayed.

When they were gone Tracker moved around behind his desk.

"Who goes first?" he asked.

"You do. When is the last time you were in Chinatown?"

Tracker shook his head and said, "Not until you tell me what this is all about."

"Do you know a man named Ah Ching?"

"Can't say that I do."

"He runs one of the gambling dens in Chinatown. He was murdered tonight."

"Why come to me about that?"

"I've told you what it's about, Mr. Tracker," Preston said. "Now suppose you answer my questions."

"Go ahead, then."

"When was the last time you were in Chinatown?"

"A couple of nights ago, with a friend."

"Who?"

"The bartender in the hotel saloon, Will Sullivan."

"The boxer?"

"The ex-boxer."

"I saw him fight a few times," Preston said, getting off the track. "He was pretty good."

"I guess he was."

Tracker decided that Preston was intelligent—and dangerous. He was trying to throw the big man off balance by letting the conversation wander.

"Do you go to Chinatown often?"

"That was the first and last time."

"You don't gamble in Chinatown?"

"I gamble, but not in Chinatown."

"Why were you there two nights ago?"

"The girl who works behind the desk is Will Sullivan's sister," Tracker said.

"Ah, the redhead," Preston said, with a very masculine glint in his eye. He was as much man as he was lawman, it seemed.

"Yes. She asked me to try and talk her brother out of going to Chinatown to gamble. She thought that it was too dangerous."

"For Will Sullivan?" Preston asked in disbelief. "Did

she think one of those little Chinamen would pick a fight with her big brother?"

"Not *one* little Chinaman, Preston."

"And speaking of fights," Preston went on, "where did you get that nasty wound on your cheek? You look as if you've been in quite a brawl."

Tracker touched his cheek as the lie sprang quickly to his lips. "Tell that to Will. He didn't appreciate my butting into his business, even though I was asked by his sister."

"Are you saying that you had a fight with Will Sullivan?"

"And came out second best, as you can see."

"I would have paid to see that," Preston said. "I understand you fought in the ring yourself not long ago."

"That was a single incident."

"Uh-huh," Preston said. "I think I know the circumstances of that incident. Seems to me you and Will Sullivan are supposed to be friends."

"We are," Tracker replied. "It takes more than a little fight to break up a friendship. I'm sure you know that."

"Yes," Preston said thoughtfully. "So you weren't in Chinatown tonight at all?"

"Your officer O'Donnell will answer that when he comes down, won't he?"

"I guess he will."

As if on cue, the door opened and Deirdre walked in leading the police officer.

Preston looked at O'Donnell, who simply nodded his head, and the chief picked up his hat.

"Mr. Tracker, it seems that your alibi has been corroborated. Still, I would appreciate it if you wouldn't plan on leaving town for a while. At least, not until I've found the murderer of Ah Ching."

"Of course, Chief," Tracker said. He also wanted to say that he was sure the death of Ah Ching would leave an empty space in the chief's wallet, but he refrained from making the comment, and the two police officials left.

"Tracker," Deirdre asked, "what the hell is going on?"

Instead of answering, Tracker sat down behind the

desk and took the whiskey bottle out of the bottom drawer.

"Pour me one, too," Deirdre said, sitting down. "We're going to stay here until you tell me what this is all about."

He stared at her, and when she refused to drop her eyes, he poured her a drink and put it on her side of the desk.

"This thing I'm working on," he began, "it took me to Chinatown the other night."

"Is that where you got hurt?"

"Yes."

"What happened?"

"Nothing. I was looking for a particular gambling hall, run by a man named Ah Ching. I didn't find it."

"And tonight?"

"Tonight I found him, and he was dead. Somebody killed him, and then set me up to be blamed for it."

"Who would do that?"

"I don't know, Dee," he said, "but I've got to find out, which is why I needed the alibi that I was here playing cards all night."

"Those people upstairs, they went along with it?"

"I guess they did."

"Why?"

"Some of them are my friends, and the rest are like me, in a way, so they went along."

"What if they hadn't?"

"They did—and you did, too. You and Shana. Why did you do it?"

She dropped her eyes then and said, "For the same reason Shana did, I suppose," but she didn't elaborate on what that reason was.

Tracker finished his drink and poured himself another one.

"What will you do now?" she asked.

"I'll go upstairs and get some sleep," he said. "First thing in the morning I'll start trying to find out who killed Ah Ching, and who set me up."

Tracker finished his second drink and put the bottle away. When he stood up, Deirdre did also, and asked, "Tracker? Can I come upstairs with you tonight?"

He smiled and said, "Sure, kid. I'd like that."

"We can go up now," she said. "Shana's gone for the evening, I think, although I'm sure she'll be looking for an explanation, too, tomorrow."

"Shana's not quite as curious and demanding as you are, Dee," Tracker said.

"What's that supposed to mean?" she demanded.

He took hold of her arms and said, "Hold on to your temper and maybe I'll explain it to you when we get upstairs."

[20]

They had made love countless times now, but Tracker's gentleness still amazed her. There were times when he took her roughly, sometimes violently, but for the most part he was very gentle with her, as he was now.

He circled her nipples with his tongue, never once letting his teeth touch them until she ached for him to do so, and begged him to. Even then, however, he ran his teeth over them easily. When he kissed her face he merely brushed his lips over her skin, and again it was she who took hold of his head and brought his mouth down roughly on her own.

She reached between them to take hold of his long, hard stalk of flesh, and her hands demanded that he mount her and enter her, which he did. He slid into her teasingly slow, until she lifted her hips in an effort to swallow all of him; then he cupped her buttocks and began to rotate her hips, slowly at first, and then faster, until her breath was shooting into his ear with every thrust.

"Oh yes, darling, yes..." she murmured, taking hold of his head so that she could thrust her tongue into his mouth. She kissed him long and hard enough to take his breath away and still would not let him come up for air. Instead, they breathed each other's breath, passing it back and forth until finally she began to tremble beneath him as her orgasm approached. She freed her mouth so she could bite her bottom lip and roll her head from side to side as the exquisite agony took hold of her, and then he was filling her up, experiencing a lovely agony of his own.

"Damnit, Tracker," she said into his ear.

"What?"

"Nothing," she said, as he rolled off of her.

"What's the matter?"

"I don't want to talk about what I was just thinking," she said, "what I almost said. I don't want to put a strain on our rel—on our partnership."

"Oh, really?" he asked. "Is that why you fight me tooth and nail on everything I want to do to the place to improve it?"

Her eyes flashed as she replied, "Improve it! You want to turn it into a gambling hall. That's not what my father and I wanted to do. We were trying to get away from gamblers and con men, and now I'm stuck with one of each."

"Which am I?"

"Duke's a con man; that's why he does such a good job of running the hotel," she said, then hastily added, "and don't you dare tell him I said that."

"I promise."

"You, though, you're a gambler."

"I never thought of myself as just a gambler," he protested.

"Yes, you are," she said, "only you gamble for higher stakes than most people. You gamble with your life."

"I think that's a little extreme—" he started to say.

"You think so? Turn over," she demanded, pushing him.

"Why?"

"Just do it."

He obeyed, turning over on his stomach.

"Look at this scar," she said, touching the one lower down on his back. "A bullet, right?"

"Right."

"And this one," she said, moving her fingers higher

93

up to a longer scar, not as puckered as the other. "A knife, right?"

"Right."

"And now your face. You'll have a scar there, too, I'll bet. Each scar signifies a time that you gambled...and won."

He turned over and looked at her.

"You're being very profound tonight."

"I'm just telling you how I feel—some of my feelings. I was hoping that you'd get interested in the hotel and stop gambling before the time came when you gambled and lost, but I guess that was too much to ask for."

"I'm not the hotel type, Dee."

"Neither was my father, and neither was I," she said. "Look at Duke. He wasn't the type either, but he's enjoying it now, isn't he?"

"Yeah, I think he is."

"He's having the time of his life. Don't let him fool you."

"You've gotten to know Duke pretty well, haven't you?" he asked.

"Yes, very well," she said. "As a matter of fact, he reminds me a little of my father. Oh, he doesn't look anything like him, but he's the same way about most things."

"I wouldn't tell him that if I were you," Tracker said. "I don't think Duke's feelings for you are exactly fatherly."

"Don't be an ass!" she snapped. "He's been nothing but a perfect gentleman since we met."

"Sure," he said. "That's what made me suspicious from the start."

"He's very fond of you, Tracker. Did you know that?"

Tracker suddenly felt very uncomfortable, and she noticed.

"You don't like that, do you? I'll tell you another one. You're fond of him, too."

"We're friends...I guess."

"And that's exactly why he'd never...never..."

"Never what?"

"Never...do anything," she said, groping for the right words. "He knows about...us."

"You've talked to him about, uh, us, have you?"

94

"No, not really."

"Has he warned you at all?"

"In the beginning he did, before I got...involved. He told me what kind of man you were."

"What kind did he say I was?"

"He said you were a good man to have on your side—if you were a man. He said that you were a little different where women were concerned."

"I guess I am."

"That's for sure, but I'd still want you on my side, Tracker."

"Thanks, honey."

"I think I'd better go now," she said, throwing back the covers, preparing to get out of bed.

"Wait," he said, grabbing her arm. "Why leave?"

"Because we're talking too much, and there are things I feel that I don't want to put into words yet."

"All right, then stay," he said, pulling her back down and covering her, "and we won't talk."

"Promise?" she asked.

"I promise," he said, and took her in his arms again.

[21]

The next morning Tracker and Deirdre were awakened by an insistent knocking on Tracker's door.

"The police again?" Deirdre asked, looking alarmed.

"Or Shana," Tracker said, joking to try and relax her. He didn't think the police would be back to him so soon.

"Bastard," she said.

"You're right," he said, getting up, "it must be Duke."

"Well, let me get something on," she complained.

"Why don't you go and take a bath?" he suggested.

"Good idea," she said, and disappeared into the bathroom.

When she had closed the door behind her, Tracker pulled on a pair of pants and went to the door.

"Who is it?"

"Duke."

He opened the door and let his friend in.

"What happened last night?" Duke demanded. "I expected you to come back to the game. Everyone did. There were a lot of questions asked last night, Tracker."

"I had to answer a few myself," Tracker said.

"Well, how about answering a few now?"

"A man was killed in Chinatown, and someone tried to get me blamed for it," Tracker explained. "That's it in a nutshell."

"I see," Duke said. "And we all alibied you for the time of the murder."

"And I really appreciate it."

"Tracker, that wasn't fair."

"Duke, I can't find out who's trying to pin a murder on me if I'm in jail. I had to stay free."

"I don't really mind," Duke said, "but what about the others? How are they going to feel when they find out?"

"Every one of them would have done the same thing," Tracker said with more confidence than he actually felt. Gamblers and lawmen just naturally didn't mix. How *would* the people at the game react when they found out that he had used them to set up a phony alibi for a murder investigation?

He was just going to have to deal with that problem later. The more pressing business at hand was finding out who killed Ah Ching. By doing that, he would also find out who had set him up to take the blame.

Tracker voiced his thoughts to Duke, who asked, "Where are you going to start?"

"Ah Ching's daughter," he said. "First, she should be able to tell me who wanted her father dead; and second, she can tell me if what I was looking for was taken from her father when he was killed."

"I guess I shouldn't even ask what that is," Duke said, "although it's not hard to guess."

"Just don't guess out loud," Tracker advised him.

"Check. Oh, I put your winnings from last night in the office safe."

"I won?"

"You barely played a half an hour, but you're five hundred dollars ahead."

"Anybody complain?"

"Doyle, but he's been complaining since the game started. I'm getting a little tired of it."

"Maybe I'll talk to him."

"Sure, in between alibis?"

"All right," Tracker conceded. "Just try and put up with it a little longer."

"Sure. Anyway, the way he's been playing, he'll be tapped out by tonight."

"Good."

"I'd better go before Deirdre gets waterlogged from waiting in the bath all this time," Duke announced.

"Deirdre?"

"Sure. Shana's on the desk, so it's either Deirdre or Angie, and Angie played poker all night."

"You're a wonderful detective, Duke."

"You're a predictable subject," Duke replied. "Look, watch your step, huh? We're kind of used to you around here."

"Get out of here," Tracker said, "before one of us starts to cry."

"I'm going, I'm going, but let me know if you need any help."

"You'll be the first, Duke."

As soon as the door closed behind Duke, Deirdre came out wrapped in a towel.

"I feel like a mass of soggy wrinkles," she complained.

"It was only Duke," he told her. "You could have come out any time you wanted to."

"Sure," Deirdre said. "You know, I don't like what you do to me, Tracker—"

"That wasn't what you said last night."

"That's not what I mean," she said quickly. "I mean, just because I...spend the night in your room doesn't mean I want...everyone to know about it."

"Duke isn't everyone, Dee."

"I know, but I have to be able to work with him. Believe me, it was okay for him to think it was me in the other room, but it wouldn't have been okay for me to come out like this while he was here."

"All right," Tracker said. "You're right. You do have to work with Duke, and you should know what's best for you in that relationship."

"I should know what's best for me in this relationship, too," she said, "but I don't."

"Can I make a suggestion?" he asked, approaching her.

98

"What?"

He grabbed hold of the top of the towel and said, "Get rid of this towel so we can do something about those soggy wrinkles."

[22]

After Deirdre dressed and went back to her own room to change, Tracker hopped into the tub himself. He had already planned his first move, which was to talk to Ah Ching's daughter. Depending on what she told him, his second move would probably be getting to see either the senator himself, or his assistant, Mark Roberts.

As he was drying off there was a knock on his door, so he wrapped a towel around his waist and answered it.

It was Duke again.

"Somebody here to see you, Tracker," Duke said.

"Who?"

"A Chinaman. I can't get anything out of him except that he wants to see you."

"Where is he?"

"In the office."

"Bring him up here."

"Right."

"And Duke—"

"Yeah?"

"Use the back stairs. I don't want anyone to see him come up here."

"Somebody is bound to have seen him come into the hotel," Duke said. "After all, it's not an everyday occurrence."

"That's why I want him brought up the back way, and let out the back way when he leaves. Got it?"

"I got it."

While Duke went down to get the Chinaman Tracker figured would be Poon, the man from Ah Ching's, he got dressed. Anna Ching must have thought it wiser to send Poon to him and arrange a meeting.

He was buckling his gunbelt on when Duke knocked on the door.

"Here he is," Duke said.

Poon was standing next to Duke, eyes on the floor, and Tracker said, "Come in, Poon."

The man looked at Tracker, and Tracker saw that he was more a boy than a man, barely into his twenties.

"Okay, Duke, thanks."

"Sure."

Tracker closed the door and turned to Poon, who was standing in the center of the room. When the boy looked up at him, he could see resentment in his eyes. Resentment for a white man? A bigger man?

"Have you got a message for me, Poon?" Tracker asked.

Poon stared at him, and Tracker wondered why Anna Ching would send Poon to him if the boy didn't understand or speak English—beyond the word "out," that is.

"Poon."

The boy didn't say anything, just extended his hand. Tracker put out his own hand, which dwarfed the boy's, and took the piece of paper that was being offered to him.

"From Anna?" Tracker asked. When the boy didn't answer, Tracker unfolded the note and read it. It was short and to the point. Anna Ching wanted him to meet her that evening at the Alhambra, which was a large hotel and gambling hall in Portsmouth Square.

"The Alhambra?" he said aloud.

Poon's face remained stoic, and Tracker assumed that he was waiting for an answer.

"All right," he said. "Tell her I'll be there."

Without acknowledging Tracker's reply, the boy started for the door, and as he opened it Tracker called out, "Go out the back way, damn it!"

He reread the note once the boy was gone, and it still said to meet her at the Alhambra. On one hand it was crazy, but on the other hand it made sense. The Alhambra catered to all kinds of gamblers, which meant men, women, foreigners—the works. They wouldn't necessarily stand out and be noticed there, the way he would in Chinatown.

Anna Ching seemed to have brains as well as beauty, and the coolness under fire to go along with it.

She was too good to be true, which made Tracker very wary of her. Still, she was the only logical first step in clearing himself, so he pocketed her note and decided to go downstairs and devote his attention to breakfast.

[23]

Duke appeared in the dining room as Tracker was fin-
ishing his first pot of coffee.

"Have a cup," he told him.

"I've had enough coffee for one morning," Duke said.
"I thought you ought to know that the police have someone watching the hotel."

"That's to be expected," Tracker said. "They must
have seen Poon—"

"Who?"

"The Chinese boy," Tracker said. "They must have
seen him come in—"

"—and not go out," Duke finished. "Maybe they'll
think he's checked in."

"Maybe." Tracker thought a moment, then asked,
"Does the cook live in the hotel?"

"Yeah. We gave him a little room—"

"Tell him to go out and buy something."

"What?"

"Anything, just so long as he goes out the front door,
and then comes back by way of the back door. Hopefully,
they won't be able to tell him and Poon apart."

"Good idea," Duke said. "I'll get on it."

"See any of the players this morning?"

"Not yet. It's a little early for them yet."

"Right. Okay, get on that cook, will you?"

"Right."

After Duke left, Tracker was about to do the same when Poker Angie walked into the dining room. He caught her attention and waved her over.

"Sit down," he said. "Breakfast is on me."

"Just some coffee and dry toast for me," she said. "Got to watch my figure, you know."

"Yeah, I saw you watching your figures last night."

"You didn't do too badly either, for someone who only played half an hour."

"Well—"

"But then, you had other things on your mind, didn't you?"

"One or two, yes," he admitted.

"Don't worry about it, Tracker," she said. "Nobody complained except for that horse's ass, Doyle."

"I heard."

"You want to tell me about it?"

"No."

"Hell, Tracker, I swore up, down and sideways that you were in that room with us last night. Don't you think I deserve some kind of an explanation?"

"You'll get one, but not now," he said.

"Okay, Tracker," she said. "I'll wait, but I don't know about the others."

"They'll wait, too."

"If you say so."

Tracker sat with her while she ate, then they got up and left the dining room together.

Under the watchful eye of Shana Sullivan, Tracker asked Angie, "What's on your agenda today?"

"What did you have in mind?" she asked.

"I've got some business to take care of."

"Well, I've got some shopping to take care of."

"Don't spend your whole bankroll," he advised.

"Don't worry," she said. "I'll be there tonight. Will you?"

"I don't know," he said, "but if I am, it'll be for more than just a half an hour. You'll get a chance to get your money back."

104

"Ha," she said. "You ain't got any of my money, friend. I'll see you later."

Tracker escorted her out and watched her walk down the street, then let his gaze wander lazily up and down the street until he spotted the policeman Chief Preston had assigned to watch the hotel—or, more to the point, to watch him. He had no doubt that if and when he left the hotel, the man would follow. When he left to meet Anna Ching at the Alhambra, he would have to use the back door. When he didn't come out the front, the policeman would have to assume that he was once again upstairs playing cards.

As long as the man didn't go up to check, he would be all right.

[24]

That evening, just as darkness started to fall, Tracker slipped out the back door of the hotel and took a round-about route getting to Portsmouth Square. When he was sure that he wasn't being followed, he went to the Alhambra.

He had worn his best black broadcloth suit, and unlike in the crowds in Chinatown, he blended into this one very nicely. He played a little faro and some roulette, just to pass the time, checking the entrance every so often for Anna Ching. He wondered if Anna would stick out here as much as he stuck out in her neck of the woods.

And then he took a good look around him.

Most of the people who frequented the Alhambra were fairly well-off, the gentry of San Francisco, and there was a fair amount of jewelry, furs, and low-cut gowns that would have attracted a great deal of attention had they been worn anywhere else. Unless Anna Ching walked in naked—and maybe not even then— she wouldn't be attracting a great deal of attention. Not in that crowd.

He was wrong.

Tracker was playing faro when a murmur went through the crowd, and he looked up to see what the attraction was.

It was Anna Ching.

She had walked in wearing a high-necked gown much like the one she had been wearing when he first saw her, only this one was plainly meant to be worn at places like the Alhambra, and not Ah Ching's in China-town. It was made of some sort of shimmering red fabric and was slit to the thigh on both sides. However, even the lovely Anna Ching couldn't command the attention of that crowd for very long, and once they'd satisfied their curiosity, they all went back to playing their games.

Except for Tracker.

He walked up to Anna Ching and said, "Hello."

"Mr. Tracker," she said. "I am glad that you could come."

Her beautiful face was expressionless and did not reflect her words at all. He suddenly found himself wondering if he could think of a way to get this girl to smile. Maybe later.

"I'm glad we could meet, Miss Ching," he said, "but why here?"

"You could not come to Chinatown," she said. "Not after last night. A man like you would be noticed right away. The police would hear of it. So," she continued, shrugging her elegant shoulders, "I come here."

"We can go into the dining room, if you like, and have some dinner," he proposed.

"That would be fine."

After they had ordered, he asked, "Did the police give you a rough time last night?"

"Not really," she said. "I acted as if the death of my father had left me dumb with grief."

"And it hasn't?"

"Death is always a possibility when you live in Chinatown, Mr. Tracker."

"Just Tracker."

"As you wish," she said.

"Will you answer some questions for me, Anna— May I call you Anna?"

"If you like, and yes, I will answer questions if they will help you find who killed my father."

"Was anything missing from your father's office after we found him last night?"

"The police asked me the same question. No, I did not find anything missing."

"Who would want your father dead?"

"Anyone who came in to gamble and lost," she answered without hesitation.

"Your father had no problems with anyone else?"

This time she hesitated, and Tracker could see that something was going through her mind.

"If I'm going to find your father's killer, Anna, you're going to have to help me."

Her lovely eyes studied him for a long time before she spoke.

"Why were you looking for my father last night? You look like a very dangerous man, Tracker. Would you have killed him if he was not already dead?"

"Anna, I had no intention of killing your father," he assured her. "I simply wanted to talk to him."

"About what?"

Tracker decided to answer her questions in the hopes that this would assure him of *her* cooperation. "A man who lost a lot of money and left his markers behind asked me to talk to Ah Ching for him."

"Why?"

"If those markers fell into the wrong hands, they could damage the man's reputation."

"He should have thought of that before he gambled."

"He realizes that. Tell me something, Anna. Aren't most of the gambling halls in Chinatown run by an organization?"

"Yes. My father was simply managing the place for the tong."

"The tong?"

"The organization you spoke of is called a 'tong.' There are several in Chinatown."

"What else do they deal in?"

"Everything. Prostitution, drugs—the opium dens are theirs, as well."

"I see. And which tong did your father work for?"

She studied him silently again and said, "You realize that you are asking me a very dangerous question."

"Yes, I do."

"We could both be killed."

"Your father has already been killed."

"I need no reminder of that," she assured him. "Very well. My father worked for the White Pigeon Tong."

"Who's the head man?"

"Loo Quon," she said, and it was almost with reverence that she spoke the name. "He is ancient, but his power is strong."

"Where do I find him?"

"Ross Alley. My father knew the exact location, but he never told me where it was."

"Did your father see him anytime before he died?"

A waiter brought their dinner to the table, and Tracker could see Anna Ching taking the opportunity to do some heavy thinking. When the waiter left, she seemed to have made a decision.

"I am going to put my life in your hands, Tracker," she said. "I did not know the name you asked me about last night."

"Royce?"

"Yes. I am aware, however, that my father was in a lot of trouble with the tong for allowing an important white man to lose heavily and then accepting the man's markers."

That had to be Royce.

"He went to see Loo Quon not too long ago and then Loo Quon sent his hatchet man, Lu Hom, to pick up some markers."

He noticed that when she mentioned the name Loo Quon, she did so with some fear in her eyes, but when she mentioned Lu Hom—whoever that was—it was with revulsion written on her entire face.

"Would the tong have killed your father over this?"

"I would not doubt it."

"Then I guess I'd better go and talk to this Loo Quon," Tracker said. It seemed that was his only recourse, now that Loo Quon was the man with the markers.

"You had difficulty finding my father," Anna reminded him. "You will find it impossible to find Loo Quon—unless he wishes to be found."

"I'll just have to try."

"Be careful of Lu Hom," she said. "He is vicious, a killer. If the tong had my father killed, it was Lu Hom who killed him."

"Would he use a knife?" Tracker asked.

That seemed to stop her for a moment.

"I admit that would be unusual," she finally said.

"Why? What weapon does he normally use."

"His hands, his feet. His body is a weapon. It is an age-old technique, which Lu Hom has perfected."

Tracker suddenly went back in his mind to the night he and Will Sullivan were attacked in that dark alley. He had been hit with hands and feet that night, but there had been no weapons at all in evidence.

Could he have had a meeting with this Lu Hom, and come away alive? If so, he was one up on the man already.

Maybe he could put that fact to good use.

Anna Ching ate her dinner without enthusiasm, and Tracker had much the same attitude. He was more concerned with the information the lovely Chinese girl had just given him, which changed his planned second move.

Originally intending to go and see either Royce or Mark Roberts, the logical move now was to find Loo Quon. Still, there was one thing that didn't feel right.

"Why would Loo Quon have your father killed? Who would he then have collect the debt? Lu Hom?"

"I do not know," Anna said. "If the *lo fan* is so important, it would make sense to me to write off the debt, but the tong do not think that way. Any debt is a matter of honor to them. They think each side should feel that the settlement of the debt is the most important thing. I do not see any sense in Loo Quon having my father killed...unless—"

"Unless what?"

"Unless Lu Hom did it on his own," she finished. "He is vicious, and likes to kill."

"Wouldn't that get him in trouble with the tong?"

"If it was not ordered, yes."

"Then maybe I should talk with Lu Hom first. Is he as hard to find as Loo Quon?"

"Perhaps not," she said after a moment.

110

"I'm going to need someone to guide me through Chinatown, Anna," Tracker said. "Would Poon do it?"

"If I asked him, yes," she said. "Poon is devoted to me...."

"Good."

"But I will not ask him."

"Why not?"

"I will guide you myself."

"That could be dangerous."

"It was my father who was killed, Tracker, not Poon's. I do not want his death on my hands. I will guide you."

"Fine, if that's the way you feel."

"My father was respected by many people in Chinatown."

"Will they help?"

"I think not, but they will not work against you if I am with you."

"Well, that's something," he said.

After dinner Tracker said, "We should go somewhere else and talk more, but I can't take you back to my hotel. The police are watching it."

"I have taken a room here," she said. "Would you like to come up?" He tried to read her invitation and see if there was anything else behind it, but it seemed innocent enough.

"That's a good idea," he said.

"Let us go, then," she said, and they both rose.

[25]

If someone had asked Tracker if he thought he would end up in bed with Anna Ching, he would have said no. He would have admitted to hoping for it, but thus far the inscrutable Chinese girl had shown no interest in such a liaison, and in fact, during the first hour they were in the room together, there was still no indication that it had even crossed her mind.

It crossed Tracker's mind, however, every time Anna Ching crossed her legs. She sat on the bed, while he sat on a hardback chair, and they made their plans for their excursion through Chinatown in search of Lu Hom and the leader of the White Pigeon Tong, Loo Quon.

It was when they had decided that it was time to leave that their eyes locked and something happened between them. Anna stood up as if to leave, but she did not move away from the bed. Tracker stood up, and instead of moving toward the door, he moved toward her. It seemed very natural as he reached for her and took her by the shoulders. In the past few seconds her breathing had suddenly gotten heavier, and her nostrils were flaring as her face flushed with the excitement she was inexplicably feeling.

112

When he closed his arms around her to pull her to him, she seemed to go limp in his arms, and simply said, "Yes."

When he kissed her, she caught fire, clawing at him while sucking wildly on his tongue. The taste and smell of the girl caused sensations in Tracker that were totally new to him. He had been with many women, and he didn't know if this one was different because she was Chinese, or simply because she was different from other women. Whatever it was, his hands worked quickly at her clothing, just as her hands worked to undress him.

Her breasts were full and round, with dark brown nipples that were swollen to an almost incredible size. He pushed her back so that she fell onto the bed, and he tumbled on the mattress with her, careful not to let his entire weight fall on her.

First his mouth sought out her breasts and nipples, sucking and chewing at them while she writhed beneath him, mumbling in Chinese.

Her skin was incredibly smooth and firm as he kissed and nipped his way down her body, pausing to lave her navel with his tongue, and then going on until his nose was nestled in her fragrant nest and his tongue was avidly seeking to taste her love juices.

His first taste of her made him eager, almost desperate, for more, and he began to run his tongue deep inside of her while she gripped the back of his head and drove her hips up in response to his pressure. Her Chinese mutterings had raised in pitch and volume until, as he found her clit and worked her toward an orgasm, she was babbling aloud.

As her belly began to tremble, he used his hands to pin her thighs to the bed, and then she stiffened as a massive orgasm seized her. Unable to move her hips, she began to drum her fists on the mattress and throw her head from side to side. Even in her frenzy, she realized that by holding her down that way, Tracker was actually increasing the intensity of her climax.

When Tracker felt her tremblings begin to decrease, he released her thighs and moved up so that his massive erection was poking at the slippery, slick portal between her legs. She spread her thighs eagerly, and

113

gasped as Tracker drove the full length of his shaft into her.

She began to mix her Chinese with a smattering of English, although the only words he was able to understand were "Oh, yes..." and "please..."

Her frenzied movements had caused her long black hair to fall across her face like a veil, and Tracker used one hand to smooth it away so that he could see her better. The look on her face was one of pure lust. As much as he was giving her, she wanted more, and gripped his buttocks in an attempt to get it. As her small hands closed over his buttocks, he slid his large hands beneath her to do the same, and from that point on, if they had gotten any closer they would have been one person.

As he continued to drive into her he realized that the sounds she was now making were not words of any language. She was simply moaning or crying out as he drove in to the hilt, and as he felt her reach her climax he increased his pace so that he went with her.

The period afterward was somewhat awkward, because neither seemed to know what to say to the other. They had both been caught by surprise, not only by the intensity of their coupling, but by the swiftness of the decision to do so.

"I did not anticipate this," Anna said, finally breaking the silence.

"Neither did I," Tracker said, "but I'm not complaining."

"Nor am I," she said, and for the first time the shadow of a smile briefly crossed her face.

The silence became awkward again and Tracker broke it by sitting up and saying, "I'd better get going. Will you go back to Chinatown tonight?"

"I think not," she answered. "Perhaps in the morning."

"Then we'll meet tomorrow near Chinatown, as we agreed."

"Yes."

She seemed preoccupied, perhaps by what had just occurred, and Tracker understood that. Neither of them spoke of it while he dressed, and after he had strapped on his gunbelt he said, "I'll see you tomorrow, Anna, and we will find the man who killed your father."

"Yes," she said again, and when there was no indication that she would say anything else, Tracker just left.

Retracing his earlier steps, Tracker took the same circuitous route back to Farrell House, where he intended to enter through the back door. As he reached for the doorknob, however, there was a shot, and only his superb reflexes allowed him to throw himself to the side, avoiding the bullet that had been meant for his back.

As the slug slammed into the wooden door, Tracker hit the ground, somersaulted, and came up holding his gun, trying to pinpoint where the shot had come from. He hoped for a second shot, so that he could pick up the muzzle flash in the darkness, but whoever had fired had apparently fled following the miss.

Tracker leathered his gun and entered the hotel without incident this time. The bullet that had been fired at him had passed through the door and embedded itself in a wall right across from it. He went to the kitchen for a knife and pried the slug loose. Dropping it into his pocket, he returned the knife to the kitchen and then went to the office, half expecting to find Duke there, at work. When he found it empty he went to the desk, dropped the slug onto it, then fished the whiskey bottle out of the bottom drawer and drank straight from it. You never get used to being shot at, and a drink always seems to help afterward.

Staring at the spent bullet, which appeared to be a large-caliber slug, he remembered what Anna Ching had said: Lu Hom never used a weapon. His body was his weapon.

So who had just taken a shot at him?

[26]

Tracker woke the next morning with two ways to go, each seemingly the right way.

First there was the White Pigeon Tong, and Loo Quon. They had the markers now, and Ah Ching, who had once had them, was dead. It made sense to think that they had killed him and tried to pin it on—what did they call him, the *lo fan?*

The second way was Arthur Royce and his "assistant," Mark Roberts. They wanted the markers back, and, considering the business they were in, probably enough to kill for them. Could it be that they had hired Tracker with just that in mind, looking for someone to pin it on? If that was the case, they were going to find out that they had picked on the wrong man.

The plan for that evening was for Tracker to meet Anna Ching just a few blocks from where Chinatown started, and from there she would try and guide him to either Lu Hom, or the tong leader, Loo Quon. The rest of the day was free, and he decided to use it to pay a visit on Arthur Royce and give him a progress report.

Royce had given Tracker his office address, where he could be reached through Mark Roberts, and Tracker found that the location was far enough from Portsmouth Square—in more ways than one—to make taking a cable car absolutely necessary.

When Tracker reached the building where Arthur Royce kept his office, he found himself facing streets unlike any others he had seen since arriving in San Francisco.

There was not a gambling hall or saloon in sight, but in spite of this, he knew that gambling of an entirely different kind still went on inside these structures: big business and politics were just as much a gamble as faro and poker—and fan-tan. Which had the higher stakes, though, depended on your point of view.

Uninvolved as Tracker was in politics, he had no idea that it was an election year until he got up to Royce's office and saw that the walls were covered with his "Vote for—" posters.

Which would make it all the easier to see why Royce and Co. had to commit murder to preserve his position.

"Can I help you?" a young man with a protruding Adam's apple asked.

"I'd like to see Senator Royce, or Mr. Roberts, his assistant," Tracker said.

"Could I have your name, please?"

"Tracker."

"Mister—" the kid began, writing it down, but Tracker interrupted him.

"Just tell one of them that Tracker is here," he said. "They'll see me."

"I'll need your full name, sir," the kid said apologetically.

"What you'll need, son, is a full set of teeth so you can announce me."

The kid's Adam's apple began to bob as he tried to swallow and stammer at the same time.

"Just do it," Tracker told him, and the kid fled behind one of the two closed doors behind him.

After a few moments, a puzzled-looking Mark Roberts came walking out and said to Tracker, "What did you say to Les?"

"Why?"

"He said there was a crazy man here to see me, and then ran out the back way."

117

"He insisted that I had to tell him my full name," Tracker said. "I didn't have time for that."

Roberts frowned, then folded his arms and said, "We're very busy up here, you know, getting ready to launch the senator's new campaign."

"That's none of my concern," Tracker said. "Is the senator in, by the way? I'd like to talk to him."

"I'm afraid you can't. He's in Washington."

"When will he be back?"

"I really can't say."

"When did he leave?"

"A couple of days ago."

"He didn't leave you any instructions when he left, did he?"

"Like what?"

"Like murder?"

"What are you talking about?"

"I tracked those markers down for you, only the man who had them is dead."

"And what happened to the markers?"

"Somebody else has them, I guess."

"Well who, damnit?" Roberts snapped. "That was your job, wasn't it? To find them?"

Tracker remained silent while Roberts stared at him, fuming, and then the assistant began to read the look in the big man's eyes as dangerous.

"I know what my job is, Mr. Senator's Assistant," Tracker said. "What I've been wondering about is yours."

"My job is to handle the senator's affairs while he tends to other, more important, matters, concerning the country."

"Keep him clean, you mean," Tracker said.

"The senator is clean."

"Except for some gambling, that is."

"Tracker, what do you want? More money? Is that it? Do you have the markers?"

"Do you?"

"What?"

"Maybe you killed Ah Ching and decided to keep the markers for yourself," Tracker suggested. "Do you have political ambitions, Roberts?"

Tracker had to admire the man for showing some backbone and standing up to him.

"Tracker, I've got work to do. If you came here to say something, then say it."

"Just this," Tracker replied. "If you and the senator tried to set me up as a patsy, you're going to find that you're dealing with the wrong man. I'll take those markers and turn them over to the nearest newspaper, and then I'll come back here for you."

"Just find those markers, Tracker."

"I'll find them, Roberts. You can count on that."

After Tracker left, Mark Roberts gave in to the weakness that he'd been feeling in his knees and sat down heavily. He was going to have to get in touch with the senator and let him know that using Tracker might not be as easy as they had first anticipated. He wished that Royce had waited until he'd been able to check Tracker out more thoroughly.

He might have to bring in more help on this.

A lot more.

[27]

It was shortly after dark when Tracker met Anna Ching
at a small hotel two blocks from Chinatown. She had
already taken a room and was waiting for him there.

When he entered the room she was waiting for him
in bed, which surprised him somewhat.

"I thought perhaps we could use the room before we
left?" she said, wearing nothing but her long black hair.

"Why not?" he asked, removing his gunbelt. "It would
be a shame to waste the room."

Afterward, as Anna lay in his arms with her hair
fanned out across his chest, he asked, "Are you frightened?"

"Yes."

"You don't have to help me, you know," he said.

"I must," she answered. "It is for my father."

No pretense that it was for him. He liked that.

"All right, then," he said. "Where do we start?"

"I think I know where we can find Lu Hom tonight,"
she said. Sitting up, presenting him with a full, unob-
structed view of the graceful curve of her back, she said,
"First we must get dressed, and then I will take you
there."

120

"In Chinatown?"

"Yes." She stood up and started to dress. "It will be dangerous."

"For you or me?"

"For both of us," she said, "but especially for you." When she turned to face him he was on his feet, reaching for his pants. "You are not Chinese," she said.

"Really?" he asked, looking down at himself. "Do you think anyone will notice?"

For the first time he saw Anna Ching smile, and her expression was like a blind woman's who was suddenly able to see.

[28]

Anna explained to Tracker that Lu Hom had collections to make for the tong that night from the gambling halls in Chinatown.

"Normally, he would have started with us," she said, meaning her father and herself.

"Why with you?"

"Lu Hom enjoyed terrifying my father," she said, as they left the hotel and started toward Chinatown.

"Just your father? Why?"

"Not just my father," she said. "He enjoys terrifying everyone, which he can do with the power of the tong behind him, but he took special enjoyment in doing it to my father."

"Why?" Tracker asked again.

They were approaching Chinatown now, and Anna said, "You will hear remarks made as we walk through Chinatown. It is because I am Chinese and you are not."

"Remarks directed at me or you?"

"Both of us," she said, "but they will be spoken in Chinese, so do not pay them any mind."

"Will you be able to do the same?"

"Words will not bother me."

Tracker believed her. It would take more than mere words to upset this girl. He remembered her reaction when they had found her father dead. Momentary shock, but she had gotten over it very quickly and had had the presence of mind to evaluate him, and then help him get away before the police arrived.

He was becoming more and more impressed with Anna Ching as the days—the moments—passed.

They walked side by side through the crowded streets of Chinatown, and Tracker could hear the remarks, the undercurrent of resentment, as the Chinese girl walked with the *lo fan*. Anna Ching held up her head, though, and displayed no shame and no discomfort. Her attitude said they could all go to hell.

She walked them to Sacramento Street, where they were refused admittance to the first gambling hall they tried.

"Now what?" he asked. "We could wait out here for him."

"No," she said. "Wait."

She knocked again, and when the eye slot opened, she spoke very quickly in Chinese, and the door opened. Whatever she had said worked as well for her as Tracker's gun had for him.

"What did you say to him?"

"Shh," she said, as the door opened.

When the door closed behind them, Tracker looked at the man who had opened it. It wasn't Poon, but it could have been.

"Is he here?" Tracker asked.

"Wait," she said again.

She spoke for a few seconds to the man who had let them in, and then he went off down the hall and disappeared.

"Now what?" Tracker said.

"Lu Hom is upstairs," she said.

"Then let's go up and see him."

"We must be careful," she said. "He is very dangerous when he has been smoking his pipe."

"His pipe?" he asked. "Oh, you mean opium?"

"Yes."

"I can't wait to see what this guy looks like," Tracker said.

"You will be surprised," she assured him. "Come."

He followed her down the hall, and then to a stairway that led up. The now-familiar odor of opium wafted down over them as they ascended, with Anna still in the lead against Tracker's better judgment. If this Lu Hom was as dangerous as advertised, it didn't make sense to him to have Anna confront him first, but she insisted that it was the best way.

"I may be the only person who can control him," she said, but when he asked why, he got the same answer he'd gotten when he asked her what she'd said to get them in in the first place.

"Sshh."

When they reached the top they came to a closed door, and Anna knocked on it. This time it was opened immediately, and after she spoke a few words to a wizened old Chinaman, they were allowed in.

Tracker didn't bother asking her what she'd said.

The room they were in was unlike anything Tracker had ever seen before. The air was thick with smoke, and the smell of opium mixed with the even stronger odor of unwashed humanity. The walls of the small room were lined with wooden cots, which were set one on top of the other, and on the cots lay men sucking on opium pipes, dreamy, faraway looks in their eyes.

Anna turned to the old man and said, "Lu Hom."

The old man chattered back at her and pointed toward the back of the room.

"This way," she told Tracker.

They walked to the back, where a large space had been cleared and a lone cot stood, with a small young Chinese man lying on it, drawing deeply on a long-stemmed pipe.

"Lu Hom," Anna said softly.

The young man turned his head and gazed dreamily at Anna, but then his pinpointed gaze hardened when he saw Tracker with her.

"The big man," he said. "Where is the other big *lo fan?* The one who was in the alley with you?"

"That was you in the alley, eh?" Tracker said, taking one step forward and stopping when Anna put her hand on his arm.

"Do not," she said. "He is dangerous."

Tracker looked at the young man again. He didn't seem to be more than twenty-four years old, and he couldn't have been more than five feet four inches tall. He certainly didn't look dangerous—until you looked at his eyes. Even if his pupils hadn't been the size of pin heads from smoking opium, they would have looked like death.

"Why did you bring him here?" Lu Hom demanded.

"He wishes to find the killer of Ah Ching."

"And you brought him here?" Lu Hom asked, looking stricken. He sat up on the cot and put his feet on the floor. "Here?"

"Look—" Tracker began, but Anna stopped him again as Lu Hom threw him a murderous gaze.

"Wait, Tracker," Anna said. To Lu Hom she said, "I brought him here so that he could see that you could not have possibly killed Ah Ching."

"What?" Tracker said, puzzled.

"He will believe me?" Lu Hom asked.

"Yes," Anna said, "if you tell him the truth."

"And why should I do that?" the tong hatchet man asked.

"Because I ask you to," Anna said.

Tracker's eyes were alternating between the two of them, and he was becoming more puzzled by the moment. Why would a man like Lu Hom do something for Anna simply because she asked him to? Was there something between them?

Lu Hom put aside his opium pipe and, in that moment, seemed to be able to throw off the effects of the drug. When he looked at Tracker, his eyes almost appeared normal.

"Ask me, then," Lu Hom said.

Tracker, still thrown by the conversation that had gone before, was prompted by Anna.

"Go ahead," she said. "Ask him."

"Did you kill Ah Ching?" he finally asked.

"I did not." Lu Hom looked at Anna and said, "There, I have answered him. Does he believe me?"

Tracker looked at Anna and asked, "Why should I?"

"You must believe him."

"Why?" he asked again.

"Because despite what he has become," she said, "my brother is a man of honor."

"Your... brother?" Tracker asked.

"Yes," she said. "Even Lu Hom, who delights in terrifying my people for the tong, would not kill his own father."

[29]

"Whoa, I'm confused," Tracker said.

"Lu Hom is my brother," she said, "although he is ashamed to admit it."

"I am not ashamed of you," Lu Hom said, "just of that old man."

"And now he's dead," Tracker said.

"And you want to find out who killed him?" Lu Hom said. "Why? He meant nothing to you."

"You're right about that, friend," Tracker said. "I was hired to do a job, and it led me to Ah Ching, and he was dead when I got there. Now somebody is trying to pin his murder on me, and that's why I want to find out who killed him."

Lu Hom stared at Tracker, then said, "You are an honest man, I see."

"I haven't always been," Tracker admitted, "but it seems the best way to go, right now."

"I have been honest with you, as well," the other man said. "I did not kill Ah Ching."

Tracker studied Lu Hom now and decided that he could believe him.

"All right," he said. "I believe you."

127

"Very well," Lu Hom said, "then you can go and leave me to my pipe."

"Not quite."

Lu Hom had started to lie down again, and at Tracker's words he stopped short and looked at the big man.

"I do not understand," he said. "I have told you what you wanted to know."

"You've told me some of what I wanted to know," Tracker said, "but not all of it."

"What else is there?"

"The markers."

Lu Hom frowned and said, "What markers?"

"You know what markers," Tracker said. "A very important white man gambled at Ah Ching's and lost heavily. He signed markers, and he does not want those markers to fall into the wrong hands."

"You are working for this 'very important' white man?"

"That's right. He's paying me to get those markers back."

"If what you say is true," Lu Hom said, "then we have entered the realm of tong business." Now he did lie back down, with his pipe in his hand, and added, "I do not discuss tong business with anyone, especially not a *lo fan*."

"Tracker—" Anna said.

"Just a minute," he told her. "Lu Hom, you took those markers from Ah Ching."

No answer.

"All I ask is that you don't let those markers fall into the wrong hands until I can buy them back."

Still no answer.

"That's not too much to ask," Tracker insisted.

When the man still didn't answer, Tracker wondered if it would do any good to draw his gun, but by then Lu Hom was once again drawing deeply on his opium pipe, gazing dreamily at the ceiling.

"I want to talk to Loo Quon," Tracker said.

Lu Hom's head turned toward Tracker, and he said, "No one sees Loo Quon."

"I'll find him."

"You cannot," Lu Hom said derisively.

"I will help him," Anna said.

128

The look on Lu Hom's face changed then as he stared at his sister.

"You cannot."

"I will," she insisted.

He turned his head sharply so that he was looking at the ceiling again, but he was not really seeing it; nor was he seeing any opium-induced dream at that moment.

Tracker and Anna waited patiently for some reply from the man on the cot, and finally he looked at them—or rather, at her—and said, "Wait to hear from me."

"About the markers," Tracker asked, "or about a meeting with Loo Quon?"

"Wait to hear from me," Lu Hom said again to his sister. He ignored Tracker completely.

Anna took hold of Tracker's arm, and the big man gave in to the pressure she was exerting and turned to leave.

"Lo fan," Lu Hom's voice said from behind him.

Tracker turned.

"If my sister is killed," Lu Hom said, still staring at the ceiling, "or comes to any harm, you will die."

"I'll remember," Tracker promised.

Lu Hom closed his eyes, placed the tip of the pipe stem into his mouth, and drew deeply.

Tracker knew how he felt. He could use a drink, himself.

[30]

The fact that Lu Hom was Anna Ching's brother—
despite the difference in names—explained a few things
for Tracker such as how she had been able to find him
so easily, and how she had been able to gain admittance.
Once they knew she was Lu Hom's sister, they did not
dare refuse. Then there was her statement that she was
the only one who could control him. Lu Hom appeared
to be loyal to Loo Quon and the White Pigeon Tong,
but apparently Anna Ching was the only person in the
world he might love.

"He hated what he considered to be weakness in our
father," she later explained to Tracker, "and so he delighted in constantly terrorizing him. Both knew that
he would never kill our father, but that did not seem
to make a difference."

"An odd relationship," Tracker said, not bothering
to mention that the same words would apply to the
brother-and-sister relationship as well.

Anna walked Tracker to the outskirts of Chinatown,
and then said, "I must go home."

"Do you—"

"Live with my brother?" she finished. "No. I lived with my father, and now I live alone."

"Would you like me to come with you?"

"Yes," she answered honestly, "but you cannot. Lu Hom would consider it dishonorable."

"Do you care what he thinks?"

"He is my brother," she said, and then added, "Besides, if you dishonored me in his eyes, he would not help you."

"Do you think he will anyway?"

"We must wait to hear from him to find out the answer to that," she said. She touched his arm and said, "So you must wait to hear from me, as well."

Covering her hand with his, he said, "I'm grateful for the help you've given me to this point, Anna."

"And I am grateful to you for wanting to find my father's killer. Now that you know it was not Lu Hom, you can look for the right person."

As he watched her walk down the street, back into the heart of Chinatown, he wondered if by absolving her brother she also thought that she was absolving the tong.

Even if Lu Hom would not have killed his father, what was to have stopped Loo Quon from having someone else do it on behalf of the tong?

And how would Lu Hom feel if that turned out to be the case?

When Tracker returned to the hotel, the poker game was in full swing, but he decided not to sit in. He wouldn't have been able to concentrate and enjoy it, anyway. Instead, he went to the office and sat behind the desk, mulling over the revelations of the evening.

He had Anna Ching's word that what her brother had said was true, that he had not killed Ah Ching; but all that meant was that *she* believed him. Well, for the moment it served Tracker's purpose to believe it as well. With Lu Hom no longer a suspect, that left Loo Quon and the tong, as well as Senator Royce and Mark Roberts.

Royce might have been stupid enough to sign some gambling markers in Chinatown, but Tracker doubted that he was dumb enough to do his own dirty work. The same went for Loo Quon. That meant that it was

131

either Roberts—or someone he hired—or someone whom Loo Quon had "assigned."

One thing was certain: Loo Quon had the markers, and getting them back was first in line. Once he had them, the killer might just come to him.

[31]

Lu Hom's heart was pounding, because he was about to do something he had never done before. He was going to ask something of Loo Quon, his master, and he did not know how Loo Quon would react.

When he entered Loo Quon's chamber, the old man looked up at him through milky eyes, and Lu once again—as he had done many times before—wondered how old his master truly was.

"I did not send for you," Quon said.

"I know that, Master," Lu Hom said. He was annoyed at how high-pitched his own voice sounded to him. He cleared his throat and said, "There is something I must speak to you about."

"What is it?"

"It concerns the death of my—uh, of Ah Ching."

"Yes?"

"There is a man who is seeking Ah Ching's killer."

"You did not kill Ah Ching, did you?"

"No."

"Then you have no worry."

"That is not my point," Lu Hom said. "This man is

also looking for the markers that Ah Ching was holding on the *lo fan* politician."

"Yes," Loo Quon said noncommittally. "Continue."

"The man says that he will pay to redeem the markers."

"Who is this man?"

"His name is Tracker."

"And what is his interest in all of this?"

"He is being paid to recover the markers before they can fall into the wrong hands."

"And what of the murder of Ah Ching? What is his interest in that?"

"He feels that someone is trying to blame him for the murder."

"I see," Loo Quon said. He frowned at his chief hatchet man and asked, "What is it you would have me do?"

Lu Hom started to speak, but his words caught in his throat.

"You may speak freely to me, Lu," Quon said. "Is your sister involved with this man?"

"She is helping him, because she believes that he can find out who killed Ah Ching."

"And what is it your sister wants me to do? Give this man Tracker the markers?"

"No, not give," Lu hurriedly said. "Let Tracker buy them back."

"I see. And is this what you would have me do, as well?"

"I would not ask you to do anything, Master," Lu said. "I told Anna I would...mention it."

"And you have," Loo Quon said. "Is there anything else?"

"The man, Tracker, would like to meet with you," Lu Hom said in a rush. He wanted to say it quickly, before he lost his courage.

"Meet with me? For what purpose?"

"I assume to discuss the terms of the redemption of the markers," Lu said.

"I have not said that I will allow him to redeem them."

"But why—" Lu began, then stopped short when he realized that he had been about to question the master. "Tracker would be acting for the man who lost the

134

money," he said instead, "and we would collect on the debt owed us."

"That is true," Loo Quon admitted, "but those markers could possibly be put to other use—better use. I have not yet decided what will be done with them."

"But—"

"I have given you ample time to express yourself, Lu," the master said. "You may go."

Lu Hom hesitated a moment, wishing that he had the courage to ask the one question that lingered in his mind.

Did Loo Quon have anything to do with Ah Ching's death?

Even thinking it while in the same room with Loo Quon caused Lu Hom's knees to turn to water, so when the old man looked up at him, he bowed and backed out of the room. He would have to tell his sister that he'd tried and failed. Loo Quon would not see Tracker.

Not willingly.

When Mark Roberts returned from the telegraph office, he sat down at his desk with the reply from the senator in Washington. Roberts had sent a telegram of his own, informing Royce that Tracker was making "uncomfortable" noises. He had then waited at the telegraph office for an answer, which was not swift in coming, and when it came, it didn't help him at all.

He unfolded Royce's telegram now and read it again: "DO WHAT YOU HAVE TO DO. Signed: AR."

That was it. Royce just dumped the whole mess—his mess—right back in Roberts's lap.

Do what you have to do, huh? That was what got them into this mess in the first place!

Roberts left the office and walked five blocks to a saloon called The Barbary.

"A beer," he told the bartender, and when the man brought it, Roberts said, "Is Dolan around?"

"Nope."

"Has he been in today?"

"Nope," the bartender said again, looking bored.

"Uh, I usually meet him here, you know," Roberts said, wondering why the man never seemed to recognize him.

"No, I don't know."

The bartender was only about five-six, but he was barrel-chested, and he had an attitude that physically intimidated Roberts.

"Uh, yeah, well, if you see him around, would you tell him I'm looking for him? I've got another job for him."

"Who's looking for him?"

"I am—uh, tell him, uh, Mark Roberts. He'll know where to get in touch with me."

"Sure."

Roberts sipped the beer, then put the mug down and said, "Thank you."

"Sure, pal."

As Roberts started to leave, the bartender said, "Hey, friend?"

"Yes?"

"You wanna pay for that beer?"

"Oh, yes," Roberts said. He was much more at ease in a bank, dickering with a bank manager, than he was in a saloon with a bartender who unnerved him. He left the money for the beer on the bar and then hurriedly left, wishing that he didn't have to deal with people like Dolan.

[32]

Before Anna answered the knock at the door, she knew who it was. She had been expecting her brother ever since the night before, after she had left Tracker.

"Come in," she said, backing away from the door.

"I would rather not," he said, but he came in anyway, warily, as if he expected to find the ghost of Ah Ching waiting for him.

"There are no ghosts here, Lu," she told him.

"So you say, little sister."

"Did you speak to your 'master'?" she asked mockingly.

"Do not mock me, or the master, Anna," he said. "It is not a safe thing to do."

"You would not let any harm befall me, older brother," she said. "I know that."

"I have no such power over Loo Quon as you think, sister," he said.

"I know," she said. "You are frightened of him."

His first instinct was to deny it, but then he said, "Yes, that is so."

Noticing his discomfort, she decided not to pursue the matter of his feelings toward his "master."

"Did you speak to him?"

"Yes."

"And what did he say?"

"He will not help your...friend."

"Why not?"

"One does not ask Loo Quon why," he said, "and if one did, he would not answer."

"What did he say?"

"He said that he had not yet decided what he would do with the markers."

"What about talking to Tracker?"

"He will not," Lu Hom said. "Loo Quon sees no one."

"No one but you."

"And a few others."

"But you can see him whenever you want, isn't that true?"

"I can see him."

She gripped her brother's arms and said, "You must get Tracker in to see him."

"That would mean not only his death, but yours and mine, as well," he said. "You may have a desire to die, little sister, but I do not."

"Lu Hom Ching—"

"Do not call me that!" he snapped, jumping back from her. "My name is Lu Hom!"

"You continue to deny our father, even after his death?"

"Yes," Lu Hom said. "He was weak—"

"—and you are strong?"

"Yes, I am!"

"Then do this thing," she said. "If not for our father, then do it for me."

"I cannot."

"You *will* not!" she snapped at him. "How would you feel if it was Loo Quon who killed Ah Ching?"

"He would not."

"Why? Because he knew that he was your father? That would not stop the master, would it?"

"Loo Quon would not—"

"Why not?"

"Why would he?" Lu Hom shot back. "What reason could he have? He already had the markers; there was no reason to kill Ah Ching."

138

"Ah Ching despised Loo Quon, the tong, and every-thing they stood for," Anna said. "That is enough of a reason."

Lu Hom shook his head and said, "No."

"Deny it," she said. "You are very good at that."

They stood frozen for a few moments, staring at each other, each waiting for a hole in the other's armor.

"You do not understand," Lu Hom said.

"I hope I never do," she said.

"You are a child," he said.

"And you are a fool," she answered, "and so am I for standing here arguing with you." She paused a moment, then said, "I will get Tracker in to see Loo Quon."

"You are mad," her brother said.

"He will see me."

"He will have you killed."

"And will you be the one to do it, my brother?"

"I will not do it," he said, "you know that. But know this as well. I will not be able to stop it."

"That is up to you," she said. "I would like you to leave now, unless you have changed your mind."

"It would serve no purpose to change my mind," he said. "Beware the tong, sister."

"If your precious tong kills me, Lu, it will then have killed all of us. You will have no family, and no friends," she said. "You might as well be dead, brother."

[33]

Tracker was in the saloon having a beer with Will Sullivan when Shana came in looking for him, wearing a worried look on her lovely face.

"Tracker."

He turned and said, "Shana. What's wrong?"

"That policeman, Preston, is here to see you," she said, "and he has two officers with him."

"Big ones?" Will asked.

"What?" she said, frowning at her brother.

"I said, are the men with him big ones?"

"Uh, yeah, they're kind of big. Why?"

"They're here to arrest you," Will said to Tracker.

"What makes you say that?"

"Why else would he bring two big men with him? To hold your hands?"

"That's silly," Shana said, but she was looking even more worried now than before.

"Maybe not, Shana," Tracker said, giving Will's words more than a little consideration. "Where are they?"

"In the office."

"That's good," Will said. "Now you can go out that way." Will indicated the batwing doors.

140

"Maybe."

Tracker walked over to the doors and got just close enough to take a peek out. Across the street he could see two big men lounging against the wall of a hardware store.

"There's two of them across the street," he said, coming back to the bar.

"And probably a couple out back," Will said.

"Well, I don't think you should try and avoid them," Shana said. "You'll be a fugitive."

"I've been a fugitive before, Shana," Tracker assured her. "Besides, I can't get myself out of this mess if I'm in jail."

"He's right about that," Will said. He looked at Tracker and said, "We've got to get you out of here."

"Not really," Tracker said.

"What?"

"What we've got to do is get *them* out of here." He turned to Shana and said, "Go back and tell Chief Preston that you couldn't find me. Tell him you don't think I'm anywhere in the hotel."

"He won't accept that," she said. "He'll look around himself."

"Let him," Tracker said. "He can't search the whole damned hotel, just my suite, and the saloon—hell, I could hide in one of the guest rooms. He's not going to search every room."

"Uh-huh," Shana said, folding her arms, "and I wonder whose room you're going to stay in?"

"Well, not Duke's, and not Deirdre's. He'll look there." He put his hands on her shoulders, turned her around, and said, "Go smile at the chief of police and tell him you looked everywhere for me but can't find me."

"But—"

"Go."

When she left the saloon, Will leaned on the bar and asked, "Whose room are you gonna hide in?"

"I'll make up my mind when I get upstairs," Tracker said. "See you later."

Tracker left the saloon and hurried through the dining room to the stairs to the second floor. As he started up he saw Shana heading for the office. When he reached the second floor, he started thinking about whose room

141

to hide in, and he came up with two choices. Either Poker Angie's or Luke Short's.

He decided to try Short's room, but when he knocked on the door there was no answer. Angie's room was at the other end of the floor, and he had to pass the staircase again. As he did, he could hear Preston saying, "I'll just check his room out, and if he's not there, we'll look around."

"Help yourself," Shana's voice called, louder than necessary he noticed and hoped that Preston hadn't.

He hurried down the hall and knocked on Angie's door, hoping she'd be there. When there was no answer he knocked again, trying not to be loud enough for Preston to hear.

As the top of Preston's shadow appeared in the hall, the door opened and Angie said, "Wha—"

"Quiet," Tracker hissed, pushing her inside and shutting the door quickly but gently behind him.

"What's going on?" she asked. "Are you that anxious to see me?"

He turned to answer her and saw that all she had on was a wet towel that was molded to her body like a second skin.

"Did I get you out of the bath?"

"No, I fell in by accident and was getting out anyway," she said.

"You shouldn't answer the door like that, lady," he said. "It might give somebody ideas."

"Oh?" Smiling at him, she unwrapped the wet towel and let it drop to the floor. Water glistened and beaded between her breasts as she asked, "Does this give you any ideas?"

"One or two," he admitted.

He reached out and touched a drop of water that was dangling from her right nipple. Since he was going to have to stay in her room for a while, they might as well pass the time pleasantly.

He pulled her wet body up against him and kissed her, pushing his tongue between her soft, full lips.

"Mmm," she moaned into his mouth. "Now I'm getting ideas," she said, reaching between them to knead his swelling column of flesh.

"What do you say we put our ideas together?" he said.

"Umm," she said, throwing her arms around him and capturing his mouth with hers.

He picked her up in his arms and carried her to the bed. He deposited her there gently, then removed his clothes and joined her.

Portions of her skin were still slick from the bath water, and right then and there she was probably the cleanest woman he'd ever tasted.

He licked the water from her breasts, then sucked her nipples until they were good and hard. After that, he continued to lick water droplets from her body wherever he could find them, and if the water drops were gold, then the black bush between her legs was a gold mine. He dug out all of those little nuggets, then tunneled in ever deeper with his tongue, until he found that one little nugget in particular.

"That's it, that's it," she cried out, "and don't you dare tease me this time, Tracker."

He was past the point of any teasing, however. He had a raging erection, and knowing that the police were looking all over the building for him while he was with Angie seemed to add even more to its dimensions.

"Oh God, yes," she cried then, "I'm coming...now!"

He sucked on her furiously, increasing the waves of pleasure that were overcoming her, and then, overcome himself by the heat of the moment, he straddled her and drove himself into her slick, hot tunnel.

"Oh, you want it today, don't you," she whispered in his ear, her hot breath adding to the fire that already burned in his loins.

"I want you," he said, and began to ride her as if she were an unbroken filly.

"Oh God, yes, Tracker," she said, "yes, yes, yes. Fill me up, please..."

She tightened her arms and legs around him, and then began to do things to him, using her muscles to clutch at his massive organ as if begging him to let himself go...and then he did, with a loud groan of pleasure, which mingled with her delighted cries. They strained against each other as if trying to change places, and they were both wet now, but with perspiration, not bath water.

143

"My God," Angie said moments later, "what got into you?"

"I guess that's what being a wanted man does to me."

"What's that mean?"

He explained about the police looking for him, and needing someplace to hide.

"So, you came to me? I'm flattered."

He didn't bother to tell her that she was his second choice.

"What other choice could there have been?" he asked.

"Let's not go into that now," she advised. "Tell me why the law is after you."

"They want me to help them solve a murder."

"And you don't want to?" she asked, surprised.

"Not the way they want me to."

"What do you mean?"

"They want me to confess."

"Confess?" she asked, frowning at him. Then, with a wry grin, she asked, "Who did you kill?"

"You mean, who do they think I killed, don't you?"

"Sorry, slip of the tongue."

"Doesn't matter," he said. "Who is not important. What's important is that I didn't do it, but I can't prove that from a jail cell."

"So here you hide, until...what?"

"Until the hotel empties of policemen," he said, then gathered her into his arms again and added, "and until I get this business of hiding right."

"I think you hide very well," she said, "but I'll be glad to help you practice until *you* think you have it right."

[34]

"Well," Duke said as Tracker entered the office, "and where were you hiding while the great search was going on?"

"I stayed with a friend. Have they gone?"

Duke nodded, but added, "Not far, though."

"Still out front and back?"

"Yes. I don't think Preston believed that you weren't here, but when he couldn't find you, he settled for the next best thing."

"Bottling me up so I can't get out," Tracker said. "Seems to be a standoff."

"Not if I know you."

"And if you don't, who does?"

Duke didn't answer, but he was pleased that Tracker had said what he did—and hoped he didn't show it.

"How is the game going?"

"The game's going fine," Duke said. "As of last night Doyle is just about tapped out, and Diamond Jack is right on his trail."

"Diamond Jack is losing?"

"Poker Angie is on a hot streak you wouldn't believe,

145

Tracker," Duke said, shaking his head. "I mean, she's so good anyway, but with this streak, she's unbeatable."

"Good for her," Tracker said. "How are the others taking being beaten by a woman?"

"Luke Short and Bat Masterson don't seem to mind," Duke said, "but they're still very much in the game."

"Must be a humdinger," Tracker said. "I'm sorry I'm missing it."

"Sit in tonight."

"Uh, no, I don't think so," Tracker said. "If I read Preston right, he'll be there tonight. The man strikes me as the type to cover all possibilities."

"You may be right about that," Duke agreed.

"I've got to forget about that game and concentrate on getting out of here tonight."

"Shouldn't be too hard," Duke said. "Not if we all work together on it."

"All?"

"Sure. You, me, Deirdre, Shana, and Will."

Tracker paused a moment, then said, "My friends."

Duke, mildly surprised, looked at the big man, then said, "That's about it."

"That's good to know, Duke, but I want to keep the others out of it."

"What about me?"

"Well...I may need you to distract the men in the back while I crawl out a window...."

"I think I can handle that."

"Good. We'll wait until after dark, and then I'll get out."

"Have you thought about what happens after that?"

"What do you mean?"

"I mean, once you get out, how are you going to get back in?"

"I'll worry about that later," Tracker said. "First I get out. If I need someplace else to hide out, I'll find it."

"I sure hope you're getting paid enough for all this trouble," Duke said, shaking his head.

"Yeah, I hope so, too," Tracker said. In fact, he thought, I hope I get paid, period.

* * *

146

"You didn't pay me enough last time," Dolan told Mark Roberts. "This time I want more."

"You were paid plenty," Roberts said.

"Not to tangle with a man like Tracker," Dolan answered.

"You know Tracker?"

"I know about him, yeah," Dolan said.

Artie Dolan was a tall man in his late thirties, with sandy-colored hair and a ruddy complexion. He was a man who would do almost any job that needed doing if the price was right.

"Five thousand dollars is a lot of money, Dolan," Mark Roberts told him.

"Yeah," Dolan said, looking around Roberts's office, pausing at the posters of Arthur Royce, "but not enough to die for. What about your boss?" he asked, pointing to a poster.

"What about him?"

"Wouldn't it be worth more than five thousand to him to make sure that nothing went wrong with his election plans?"

Inadvertently, Roberts's eyes moved to one of the posters, then back to Dolan.

"I don't know what you—"

"Hey, friend," Dolan said, "I didn't start in this business yesterday. You don't have the kind of money we're talking about, and your boss does. He's trying to buy this election, and that's fine with me. I don't vote, anyway. If he doesn't want to pay, then you can get someone else."

Dolan started to get up, and Roberts said, "Wait a minute."

Dolan sat back down and waited.

"All right," Roberts said, "ten thousand."

"Twenty-five."

"What?"

"Tell me your election budget won't cover that," Dolan suggested.

Roberts drummed his fingers nervously on the desk top. This whole business was starting to get to him. He could feel himself unraveling, coming apart at the seams.

"Okay, all right," Roberts said, "but five now and the rest after you've done the job."

"You got a deal, friend," Dolan said. He smiled, show-ing tobacco-stained teeth, and said, "See, that wasn't so painful, was it?"

Roberts took the money out—he'd already gotten together five thousand dollars—and handed it across the desk.

The gunman tucked the money away, stood up, and answered his own question.

"Didn't hurt any more than having a healthy tooth pulled, right?" He turned to the smiling face of Arthur Royce on one of the posters and said, "Ain't that right, Senator?"

[35]

Tracker was in Duke's room, waiting for darkness so he could sneak out of the hotel, when there was a knock on the door.

He moved to the door and asked, "Who is it?"

"Tracker, it's Deirdre."

He opened the door and said, "Come on in, Dee."

She stepped into the room, and he checked the hall and then closed the door.

"Duke told me what you're planning to do," she said.

"Oh, he did, huh?"

"Yes. Don't be mad at him, though. I made him tell me."

"You can be pretty persuasive sometimes, Dee," he said. "I know that, but if you came here to talk me out of it, forget it. Like I said before—"

"I came to offer my help," she said.

"What?"

"I know you didn't kill anyone, Tracker," she said, "and I want to help you prove it."

He reached for her and pulled her close, holding her tightly against him for a moment, then releasing her and holding her by the shoulders at arm's length.

149

"I appreciate the offer, Dee. Now why don't you get out of here and take care of some hotel business."

"I want to help you."

"You already have, Dee, believe me, but I don't want you to get involved."

"I'm already involved."

"With me, yes," he said, "but not with the police. I'm sorry, but that's that. Go to your room, go do something in the kitchen, but keep yourself busy for the next hour or so, and the next time you see me, everything will be okay."

She stared at him a moment, then said, "I only hope that the next time I see you, you're not behind bars...or dead."

"I promise, Dee," he said, holding up his right hand, "neither one."

"You promise, huh?"

"Word of honor."

She put her arms around his waist, hugged him, then let him go and headed for the door.

"I don't know what I'd do without you in my life, Tracker," she said, "but it's times like this that sometimes make me want to try it and see."

Tracker smiled, and as the door closed behind Deirdre he said, "I'm sorry I can't say the same, Dee."

[36]

Getting out was relatively simple, and it was Duke's decision to use Deirdre after all.

"I told you—" Tracker started to protest, but Duke cut him off and explained his logic.

"Who would be more distracting to you as a man— me carrying a couple of plates of food, or Deirdre?"

"I get the feeling you just don't have confidence in the hotel food," Tracker said.

"I'm just hedging the bet, that's all."

"All right," Tracker agreed, "we'll do it your way, but stay close by her, okay?"

"Tracker, she's in no danger from two policemen— but okay, I'll be close by."

Duke's room was on that side of the hotel, so Tracker went up there and peered cautiously out the window, without having lit a lamp. He was able to make out the shape of the two policemen on the darkened back street. After a few moments, a door from the hotel opened, bathing the street in light, and then Deirdre appeared, carrying a tray with two plates of food. He waited until she had engaged them in conversation, then slowly slid open the window. Keeping a wary eye on the three people in the street, he swung his long legs out the window, turned, and then suspended himself by his hands and waited for the right moment.

His hands were beginning to tire, when there was a sudden burst of laughter from the two policemen, and Tracker released his hold on the windowsill.

He dropped to the ground much more heavily than he had anticipated and the jarring pain in his knees caused him to grunt aloud.

"What was that?" he heard a man's voice call out.

"I didn't hear anything," Deirdre's voice answered.

"No, I heard it, too," a second man's voice said.

Tracker stood up and started running, and behind him he heard both men starting to shout.

"Somebody dropped from a window!"

"Stop! Stop or we'll shoot!"

The threat added speed to Tracker's legs and helped him ignore the soreness in his knees. As he turned the corner onto the main street, heading away from the hotel, he heard a shot, and the slug buried itself in the wall of the building.

On the main street, he ran without looking back, and turned into the very next alley he could find. Flattening himself against the wall, he waited until one of the policemen had run past him, and assumed that both men had split up in order to cover more ground.

He walked to the back of the alley, which was closed off by a high wooden fence, but with his height he was able to reach the top and scale the wall.

Will Sullivan was waiting on the other side.

"Jesus," Tracker said when he saw Will.

"Take your hand away from your gun, boss," Will said.

"You scared the shit out of me!" Tracker complained.

"Sorry, boss."

"What are you doing here? What made you think I'd come this way?"

"Oh, I don't know," Will said. "I just ran the same route and figured this was the way I would come. I meant to have your horse waiting, but the police have him covered, and I couldn't get another one."

"That's okay," Tracker said, "I'd just be easier to see if I was riding a horse."

"Oh," Will said, sounding disappointed, "I guess it wasn't such a good idea, huh?"

"Will," Tracker said, putting his hand on his friend's shoulder, "thanks for wanting to help. I appreciate it."

"Sure."

"But get lost now."

"What?"

"I can't say it any plainer, Will."

"I want to help, boss—"

"I know; everybody wants to help," Tracker said, "but, Will, this is what I do."

"Run from the law?"

"I'm familiar with situations like this, Will," Tracker amended. "I know what I have to do, and I can't do it with you—or anyone else—along to hold me back."

"I'm not trying to hold you back—"

"Damnit, Will!" Tracker snapped. "I don't have time to stand here and argue with you. I can move better on my own, and that's all there is to it. Go back to the hotel, please?"

"All right, all right," Will said, "don't get sore. I'll go."

"Hey," Tracker said, "I'm not going to run into your sister along the way wanting to help, am I?"

"No, I told her to stay put, that you didn't need her along to slow you—" Will stopped himself short when he realized what he was saying, then grinned at Tracker and said, "Okay, boss. But take care, huh?"

"I intend to."

Tracker started down a branch of the alley and onto a side street, and then began to work his way in a circle until he could reach the other side of Portsmouth Square, where he'd catch a cable car to Chinatown. The problem facing him now was what to do when he reached there. He didn't know how to find Anna, so whatever he did he was going to have to do without a guide.

He remembered what he had told Will about having been in situations like this before. Sure, he knew exactly what he was doing, stumbling around the darkened streets of Chinatown with no idea where he was going.

Still, the way things were in Chinatown, word should get around pretty quick that he was looking for someone—or something, and maybe he'd get lucky. Maybe someone would come looking for him, someone who could lead him to Loo Quon, because he had his doubts about Lu Hom being able to get him in to see the tong leader.

The young man was likely to be just a puppet to the powerful leader of the White Pigeon Tong, whether he knew it or not, and when he ceased to be useful, he would very probably cease to be.

However, that was academic, because even if Lu Hom had been able to get Quon to agree, Tracker wouldn't be able to find *him,* either.

His only plan at the moment was to walk around Chinatown and ask a lot of questions, and hope that his course would bring someone out of the woodwork.

Someone he could handle, and turn the tables on, before they could kill him.

[37]

Tracker spent hours walking up and down the streets of Chinatown. Every time he came to a particularly congested street, a path would suddenly open up before him, then close behind him. No one ever said a word to him, and his several attempts at asking questions proved fruitless. Either they didn't understand him, or they simply did not wish to.

As if by design—but quite by accident—Tracker found himself on Sacramento Street, where Will and Anna had already taken him. He would have found his own way there if he could have, but all of the streets in Chinatown—especially after dark—seemed to look alike.

Once he was on Sacramento Street he started to look for the door to the place where he and Anna had found Lu Hom. Maybe by presenting himself there he might prompt someone to take some kind of action and save him from any more wandering about.

When he finally found the door he wanted, he knocked, and when there was no answer he took out his gun and used the butt to knock again, loudly and insistently.

When the eye slot opened and a pair of eyes appeared, Tracker repeated the process that had gotten him into Ah Ching's gambling hall. He pushed the barrel of the gun through the slot and ordered the man on the other side to open it. When the man hesitated, he cocked the hammer of his gun for effect, and the door opened.

Ignoring the man once the door was open, Tracker hurried down the hall to the stairway that led up to the opium den. When he reached the top he pounded on the door until it was opened, then pushed his way in.

Making a snap decision, Tracker fired two shots into the ceiling and started shouting for everybody to get out. In seconds the place was swarming with little Chinamen rushing for the door, chattering at the top of their lungs. For good measure Tracker began kicking over some of the cribs, which caused the man in charge to rush at him, grabbing his arm and shouting in rapid-fire Chinese.

Tracker holstered his gun and gathered the man's shirtfront into his big fist, virtually lifting the man off the floor.

"Lu Hom," he said into the man's face.

The man simply continued to rattle on in his native tongue, and Tracker was sure that nothing complimentary was coming out. He shook the man until the torrent of Chinese epithets stopped, and then said again, "Lu Hom."

He didn't actually expect any kind of answer; he just wanted to impress upon the man that the reason he had done all of this was to find Lu Hom. With that done, he dropped the wriggling man to the floor and started down the steps. At the foot of the steps it was congested with people, but not all of them were trying to get out. Some of them were looking up at him, and there was no fear or confusion on their faces.

Gradually, as the crowd thinned out, he realized that there were about a half dozen men down there, waiting for him to come all the way down.

"Now just hold it," he said, stopping halfway down the steps. "I'm looking for Lu Hom."

Six faces stared up at him without expression, and

156

then the man in front started up the steps, followed by the others.

"Wait!" Tracker said, and when that did no good he pulled out his gun and pointed it at them. "Stop!"

But they didn't stop. They just kept coming up the steps at him. Tracker fired one shot into the steps in front of the lead man, but that didn't stop them, either.

"Damnit!" he said, and after a split second of hesitation, he made his decision and shot the lead man in the right thigh.

The man screamed, clutched his thigh, and went down, but behind him the other men bulled past him and continued to approach Tracker. He cocked the hammer on his gun, and then decided that he couldn't just stand there and shoot them all down. He turned and went back up the stairs into the opium den and shut the door behind him. He looked around and found a thick chunk of wood, which he jammed against the wall and floor, pinning the door shut. It wouldn't hold forever, though, and he was going to have to find a way out of there. He fired a couple of shots through the door, hoping to slow them down a bit, then began looking for a back door or a window. It soon became apparent that the room had neither. As an opium den, it could not afford to have windows, but he had been almost certain that there'd be a back door. Now that there wasn't, it looked as if he was stuck. There was no way out, and the door wasn't going to take too much more of a pounding from the people outside.

It looked as if his plan had worked...all too well.

[38]

Tracker made one more circuit of the room, looking for a way out, and as the door started to splinter he heard something that made him stop. He began banging his heel on the floor. One particular spot sounded different from the rest. He crouched down and, sure enough, found what appeared to be a trapdoor. Finding a fingerhold, he pulled the door up and saw that it led to the room below, the one used for gambling.

He sat with his feet dangling and held the door in such a way that, once he dropped through, it would shut behind him. Maybe he'd get lucky and none of the men that were after him would know about the door.

He heard a loud crack and saw an arm poke through the door of the room, and he knew that now was the time. He dropped through the trapdoor and struck the floor below with a bang. His knees, which had already been jolted once that night, buckled, and he fell sprawling, but relatively unhurt. Looking up, he saw that the door had indeed shut behind him, and he could hear the pounding feet of the men who had obviously broken into the room.

He regained his feet and headed for the door that

led to the hallway. Once in the hall he decided against taking the chance of going out the front way and went in the other direction, where there had to be a back door.

Knowing it was only a matter of minutes before the men upstairs realized that he was gone, he hurried down the hall, trying doors on either side until he found the right one, a door that led to an alley behind the building. He stepped through, shut the door behind him, and for a brief moment felt that he was safe.

"You seem to have gotten some people mad at you," a voice said from his left. He turned quickly, but found himself looking down the barrel of a gun. The man holding the gun was a tall, scruffy-looking guy in his late thirties.

"Tracker, isn't it?"

"And if it is?"

"Then I've got the right man," Dolan said.

"For what?"

"For what I have in mind. Hand over your gun— and use your left hand, if you don't mind?"

Tracker reached across his body with his left hand, lifted his gun from his holster, and handed it to the man, who tucked it into his belt.

"Good. Now, suppose we get away from here before your friends come down."

"My friends," Tracker said, looking up for a moment.

"Yeah, they won't treat either one of us very well if they find us," Dolan said.

"Oh, you mean you're not with them?"

"I'm with myself, friend," the man said. "Now let's move. I want to find someplace nice and quiet so we can talk."

"About what?"

"You want to go into that here?"

Actually, Tracker wouldn't have minded. He had the feeling that he was better off with the five unarmed men upstairs than the one with the gun downstairs.

"Yeah, maybe you do," Dolan said, "but I don't; so let's move along, Tracker, before I put a bullet in you right here."

[39]

Dolan walked Tracker for a couple of blocks. The gunman had holstered his gun so as not to attract any more attention than they already were. Tracker had no doubt that Dolan would be able to get his gun out before he could make a move against the man.

"Do you know where we're going?" he asked after they'd gone another block.

"To tell you the truth, I don't," Dolan said. "I'm just looking for a nice, quiet, dark corner."

"You mind telling me who you are while we're looking?"

"Nobody you ever heard of," Dolan said, "although I've heard of you, all right."

"You have, huh?"

"Sure. You got quite a rep as a tough man, though you don't seem too tough at the moment."

"Give me back my gun, or get rid of yours, and we'll find out," Tracker suggested.

"I'd like to, Tracker, I really would, but I've got too much riding on this to take any chances with you. Hold it," the man said suddenly.

"What?"

"Down this alley."

Tracker looked to his right and saw a dark alley, barely wide enough to accommodate two men walking side by side.

"In there?"

"Don't stall," the man said, and Tracker heard the sound of the man's gun being drawn. "Move."

"What's your argument with me, friend?"

"I don't have a thing against you, Tracker," the man said. "This is strictly business."

"Like shooting at me behind the hotel the other night?"

"Exactly."

"Who sent you?"

"Never mind," Dolan said. They were in the alley now, and he added, "Turn around."

"Why?" Tracker asked, doing so. "Got something against shooting people in the back?"

"As a matter of fact, I do."

"What's the difference? Murder is murder, isn't it?"

"This ain't murder, it's business. I told you that.... And speaking of business, where are the markers?"

Tracker hesitated, then said, "In my pocket. I got them back, so you don't have to—"

"Stay still, Tracker," Dolan said, "and maybe it'll hurt less."

"Hey, wait. I've got the markers, I said. I'll give them to you—"

"That's okay," Dolan said, "I'll just take them off of you...after."

"Hold it," Tracker said, "I don't have them on me—"

"This is just business, Tracker," Dolan said, "but I really don't have any choice."

Dolan cocked the hammer on the gun, but as he was about to pull the trigger, something struck him in the back, causing the shot to go wild. The man's eyes popped as he was propelled forward toward Tracker, who sidestepped and let the man go on by. Dolan fell to the ground, but before Tracker could make a move, someone rushed past him and got to the fallen man first.

It was Lu Hom.

Tracker watched as Lu Hom disarmed Dolan with a well-placed kick, then plucked Tracker's gun from the

161

man's belt and tossed it to him, turning his back for a moment.

Dolan, trying to take advantage of Lu Hom's back, struggled to his feet and launched a punch at the Chinaman, but before Tracker could even shout a warning, Lu Hom pivoted, caught Dolan's hand, and then struck Dolan quickly and efficiently on the jaw. The man keeled over and fell to the ground, unconscious.

"You are unhurt?" Lu Hom asked, turning to Tracker.

"Thanks to you," Tracker said. "Where did you come from?"

"I heard about the tall *lo fan* who was searching all over Chinatown for me. It was not hard to guess who it was."

"I see."

"I saw this man take you away from Willie Moi's opium den and followed. Who is he?"

"I'm not sure," Tracker said. "All I know is that he was going to kill me."

"Perhaps we should find out why?"

"That might be a good idea—" Tracker started to say, but behind Lu Hom he saw Dolan moving, picking his gun up from the ground and bringing it to bear on Lu Hom's back. "Behind you!"

Lu Hom's reaction was purely by reflex. He pivoted on his right foot, raised his left, and then, in a pistonlike movement, drove it into Dolan's jaw. The gunman's head was thrown back, and with an audible crack, his neck snapped.

As Dolan slumped to the ground again—for the last time—Tracker stepped up next to Lu Hom and said, "Well, I guess we won't be able to ask him."

"I am sorry," Lu Hom said. "I acted out of reflex."

"That's okay," Tracker said, going down on one knee. "Maybe I can find something to give us a hint."

Quickly going through the dead gunman's pockets, Tracker found a stack of money which, when counted quickly, amounted to five thousand dollars.

"Well, this tells me one thing."

"What?"

"Killing me wasn't his idea," Tracker said, showing Lu Hom the money. "Somebody paid him to do it."

"Who?"

162

"I'm not sure," Tracker said. "There are a lot of possibilities. How about Loo Quon?"

"Never."

"Why not?"

"The tong would not hire a *lo fan* to do its killing."

"That's right," Tracker said. "They use you, don't they?"

"If you will remember," Lu Hom said, "I just saved your life."

"Which only confuses me more. Why did you?"

"I am not sure of that myself," Lu Hom said, "just as I am not sure that what I am going to do next is the right thing to do."

"What's that?"

"Come with me," he said, "and I will take you to see Loo Quon."

[40]

Tracker didn't know why, but he believed Lu Hom. He could easily have believed that Anna's brother was leading him into a trap, but he didn't.

"Why are you doing this?" he asked as they traveled the dark, crowded streets. Tracker noticed something different, though. Now that he was traveling with Lu Hom, he was no longer getting looks from people. In fact, they seemed to be striving to avoid looking at the two of them.

"I do not know," Lu Hom answered.

"Is it for Anna?"

"My sister is a foolish girl," he said. "She would risk her life to find the man who killed her father."

"Your father, too."

"Do not remind me of that."

"I'm sorry."

"I will do what I must to keep my sister from being hurt," Lu Hom said, "and I will discuss my reasons no further."

"Fine with me," Tracker said. "Let's just get it over with."

Lu Hom led Tracker to Ross Alley.

"Stand back, away from the door," he instructed Tracker. When the big man obeyed, Lu Hom knocked on the door. The eye slot slid back, and then the door was opened. Lu Hom entered, and the door closed behind him, leaving Tracker alone on the street.

Five minutes passed, then ten, and Tracker began to wonder. After fifteen minutes he was about to make a move, when the door opened and Lu Hom looked out and beckoned him.

"Inside."

Tracker moved in quickly, and Lu Hom closed the door.

"Why do all these places look alike?" Tracker asked in a low voice.

"It is the most efficient way."

Tracker started down the hall, but Lu Hom said, "Wait. I must go first, or no door will open."

"Be my guest."

"We must go down."

"Down?"

"Loo Quon feels safer underground. He has many enemies."

"I can imagine."

"Come."

Tracker followed the smaller man down the hall, looking behind him every few steps. A nagging doubt about Lu Hom's sincerity was still unavoidable, and it kept him careful.

"If anyone questions us, just keep silent," Lu Hom said.

"I wouldn't know what to say, anyway."

Finally they reached the door Lu Hom wanted, but before opening it he turned to face Tracker.

"You must not speak to Loo Quon."

"What good is getting to see him if I can't talk to him?" Tracker asked.

"If you speak to him before he gives his permission, you will be risking his wrath."

"I'll risk it."

Shaking his head, Lu Hom said, "You are either very brave or very ignorant."

"Ignorant, most likely," Tracker said. "Let's go."

165

Lu Hom opened the door, and they started down the narrowest, longest stairway Tracker had ever seen.

"A long way down, isn't it?"

"Yes," Lu Hom said, "almost to the very bowels of the earth. It was once used to hide smuggled goods."

"I'll bet."

Finally, they reached the bottom and another door.

"Is Chinatown all locked doors?" Tracker asked, expecting no answer.

Lu Hom touched the door, and it swung inward on rusty hinges that squeaked. Tracker could see that the door was made of thick oak and would probably have withstood anything short of dynamite.

The room inside was totally dark, except for a small spot of light in the center of the room. The light came from a candle that was sitting on a small table, and at the table, seated cross-legged on the floor, was the oldest-looking man that Tracker had ever seen, white, Chinese, or otherwise.

"Is that—"

"Quiet!" Lu Hom hissed.

Tracker kept quiet.

"Stay here," Lu Hom whispered.

Tracker watched as Lu Hom took small, almost mincing steps toward the old man. He said something in Chinese, but the old man did not answer, nor did he look up.

"Loo Quon," Tracker heard Lu say in a louder voice— or maybe it just sounded loud because of the cavernous room they were in. At least, it sounded cavernous. The light from the candle did little more than light the old man and his small desk.

"Loo Quon," Lu said again, followed by something else in Chinese.

Tracker examined the seated man from where he was and came to the conclusion that the man was dead. His head was down on his chest, and he continued to resist any of Lu Hom's verbal efforts to get his attention.

"He's dead," Tracker said.

"What?"

Tracker started forward, walked past Lu Hom, and approached the old man.

166

"Do not touch him!" Lu Hom shouted, sounding panicky.

"Don't worry," Tracker said. "I told you, he's dead."

"That cannot be."

Tracker leaned over the body and touched the man's neck, which felt like brittle parchment. He put his hand against the man's chest and pushed so that he sat up straight, then let him go, and the body slumped over again.

"He's dead."

"But—that cannot be," Lu Hom said, aghast. "He cannot be dead. He is Loo Quon, master of the White Pigeon Tong."

"And he can't die?"

"How did this happen?"

"Well, no marks on the body," Tracker said, "and he's an old man. I'd say he just up and...died. When's the last time you saw him?"

"Yesterday."

"Then I guess he could have died sometime yesterday or today. Does—did he ever leave this room?"

"Never."

"What about food?"

"He ate one meal a day, at night, and I brought it to him. He did not eat yet tonight."

"Well then, that's it. He died of natural causes."

"This is—incredible," Lu Hom said.

"No it's not," Tracker said, turning to face Lu Hom. "That's life. Where would the markers be?"

"I do not know."

Tracker turned back to the desk, went through some of the little drawers.

"That's it," Tracker said, straightening. "Let's go."

"Where?"

"Let's get out of here," Tracker repeated. "I assume that the tong has some other men in this building?"

"Of course."

"Will it be any easier for them to believe that Loo Quon died of natural causes than it is for you?"

"Harder," Lu Hom said. "They have no imagination."

Lu Hom seemed to have recovered from the shock

167

very well. Tracker wondered if a man whose body was a weapon could kill another man without leaving any marks.

It was something to think about.

Epilogue

Lu Hom and Tracker got out of the building without running into any of the tong's "unimaginative" men, and then split up.

"I must go to Anna and talk," Lu Hom said. "With Loo Quon dead, I must reevaluate my position."

"I hope you make the right decision," Tracker said, "for the both of you."

Lu Hom left without a word after that, and Tracker never saw him—or his sister—again.

Tracker went to an entirely different neighborhood, looking for Mark Roberts. He figured that Roberts would still be in his office, waiting for the sandy-haired man to come back to report that he'd done the job and collect the rest of his money.

When Tracker tried the door to the office, it opened, and a voice from inside said, "Dolan?"

"Dolan's dead," Tracker said, stepping in. Roberts was sitting at the desk where the kid with an Adam's apple had been sitting, and when he saw Tracker, he stood up and backed against the wall.

"Tracker!"

"I brought the markers," Tracker said, approaching the desk.

"Oh, yeah?"

"I'd like to get paid."

"Uh, we didn't settle on a price—"

"Just give me what you owe Dolan. He won't be needing it."

"Dolan?"

"Don't play games with me, Roberts," Tracker said. "I'm not in the mood. Get the money."

"It's—it's in the other office."

"Let's go."

Roberts hurried to the other office, and Tracker followed. The man went around behind the desk and started to open the top drawer.

"If you come out of that drawer with a gun," Tracker said, "you'll never live to see another election."

Roberts froze, passed his hand over the gun in the drawer, and picked up the four packets of money. He took them out and put them on the desk, and they matched the one in Tracker's pocket.

"Fine," Tracker said, moving the money to his side of the desk, and then stuffing it in his pockets.

"The markers?"

"I have them."

"C-can I have them?"

"Sure, but first we're going to take a ride on a cable car."

"To where?"

"That's up to you," Tracker answered. "We can go see Chief Preston, or we can take a one-way ride—for you, anyway."

"What are you talking about?"

"Put your hands up over your head."

"Why?"

"Because if you don't, I'll shoot you."

Roberts obeyed, and Tracker searched his pockets, coming up with a brief telegram.

"From the senator, huh?" Tracker asked. He read it, then said, "I see that you take your instructions literally."

"What do you mean?"

"First you sent Dolan to get the markers from Ah

170

Ching, and he killed him. You expected him to kill him—with me the flunky—but you didn't expect him to come back without the markers. You must have thought I had them, and you sent Dolan to kill me and get them."

"That's—"

"Don't bother," Tracker said. "Let's go see the chief of police and you can explain it all."

"Tracker, I'll pay you—"

"I've already been paid," Tracker said, patting his pockets. "Let's go."

"But—but what about the election?"

"Well, you and the senator were afraid these markers were going to fall in the wrong hands, weren't you?" Tracker asked. He took the markers out of his pocket, held them in his hand, and said, "I suggest you send a telegram and tell him that they did."

Back at the Farrell House, Tracker asked Deirdre, "Is the game still going on?"

She turned and stared at him from behind the desk. "What are you doing here? The police—"

"The police have been satisfied of my innocence," he told her. "What are you doing behind the desk?"

"Shana had a fight with Will and left. I think she quit."

"Again?" he said. "I'll talk with her tomorrow. What about the game?"

"It's still going on, as far as I know," she said. "Tracker, what happened?"

"I finished my job," he said, "and got paid. Now I can concentrate on poker."

"I see," she said. "And that's the only explanation I get."

"Why don't you wait for me in my room and I'll think of something else to tell you . . . after the game."

"If you think that I'm going to wait for you in your room while you're playing poker—"

"Okay," he said, kissing her on the cheek. "Wait in yours."

He went upstairs, thinking how ironic it was that he was going to play poker with the money that had been paid out to take his life by a politician who had taken the biggest gamble of his life—and lost.

TRACKER

TOM CUTTER

This adventure series features Abel Tracker, a 6'4",
cardplaying, hardfisted, womanizing, ex-bounty
hunter who is as handy with a gun as he is with
his fists.

THE WINNING HAND, Tracker #1
83899-0/$2.25
When Tracker becomes the owner of a San Francisco
hotel after winning a high-rolling poker game, he
finds himself caught up in a boxing match with
Kid Barrow and entangled with three pretty women
and two of the deadliest gunfighters in California.

LINCOLN COUNTY, Tracker #2
84152-2/$2.50
Tracker continues to brawl with the best gunfighters and indulge his appetites with the most
beautiful women in the West. In his latest adventure,
bullets come after Tracker faster than women—when
he has to teach some manners to Billy the Kid.

___

AVON Paperback Originals

___

Available wherever paperbacks are sold or directly from the publisher. Include $1.00 per
copy for postage and handling; allow 6-8 weeks for delivery. Avon Books. Dept BP, Box 767,
Rte 2. Dresden, TN 38225.